THE DRAG TATTOO

BLUEWATER COAST: BOOK 1

Roxie Ray

© 2020

Disclaimer

This is a work of fiction. Names, places, characters and events are all fictitious for the reader's pleasure. Any similarities to real people, places, events, living or dead are all coincidental.

This book contains sexually explicit content that is intended for ADULTS ONLY (+18).

Contents

Prologue - Anthony

The room was full of dragon shifters and humans, mingling uncomfortably. My parents had done exactly as I'd asked, thank goodness. The decorations weren't over the top, and they'd even hired a DJ.

My best friend's voice cut through my introspection. "Give it up!"

I looked around, searching for Skye. I'd been looking for her for half the party. I hadn't seen her since it started, but I'd been pulled aside several times by members of my clan, congratulating me on my sixteenth birthday.

Normally these parties were clan only, but I'd insisted my human friends be invited as well. We lived as humans, in a human town, working jobs with them and going to school with them. It wasn't fair that I couldn't have all my friends at my party. When I'd put my foot down, my parents had caved.

That gave me hope for the future of my parents' acceptance of humans. I needed them to be open-minded.

Moving around the large rec room, I smiled and talked to clan members. Several wished me luck on my upcoming first shift, though they did it quietly, so they didn't freak out the human guests. I hoped this party would help with all the humans in Bluewater Coast thinking our clan was some sort of religious cult.

Our clan knew about the rumors. That's what made them stick so close together, ironically. They should've mingled more with the townsfolk instead of avoiding them. They'd made their own beds. I was going to be alpha someday, and Dad was always telling me to start thinking like one. So, I'd put my foot down about the party.

If I hadn't been able to invite my best friend, Skye, I would've been pretty upset. I lost track of her voice as I moved around the room, so I opened my senses to seek her out. She was always easy for me to find, filtering out everyone else until her annoyed voice reached my ears. "Will you find someone else to bug?"

"But I like bugging you." Jace's voice bugged *me*. I rounded the corner to find Skye leaned against a wall with Jace beside her. I had to force myself not to growl at him. He had his arm up by her head and his typical cocky smile plastered on his smug face.

"Shove off." At least I kept my voice out of a growl, but Jace definitely heard the warning. He didn't mean any harm, but I couldn't stand him being in Skye's space.

Jace gave me a confused look but laughed. "Whatever, Ant." He shot Skye a sly look. "See ya later."

She gave him a finger-wave as she shook her head. I was glad she found him annoying. It would've all been much worse if she'd found his flirtations charming.

I didn't speak for a few moments as Jace crossed the room. Another member of our clan, Tessa, stopped him. They spoke for a few seconds before both of them looked at me and Skye. When they saw I already had my gaze on them, they looked away very quickly.

So Jace had picked up on the threat in my voice. What a gossip he was. He hadn't waited a full minute before blabbing.

"So." I turned back to Skye and put my clanmates out of my mind. We'd been raised together, having been born around the same time. They'd give me plenty of shit about this later, I wasn't going to worry about it right now. "Are you having fun?"

She shrugged. "I guess. It's a little annoying, seeing all the catty girls vying for your attention."

I agreed with that. I didn't care for the fake girls at our high school, but I'd wanted the party to be open for everyone in town, so of course, they'd come. They followed me around campus, too, every chance they got.

"How about we go dance and take your mind off the jealous girls."

Skye turned her big green eyes up and stared at me with a smirk on her face. "I don't see that they have much to be jealous of, but sure. Let's dance."

I wanted to take her hand, but we didn't have that sort of relationship, as much as I wished we had. If those other girls knew how I really felt about Skye, they'd have more than enough to be jealous of.

When we got to the middle of the dance floor, I put my hands on her hips and thanked my lucky stars that the music had slowed to something we could sway to, instead of me trying to look cool dancing to a fast song.

With every movement of our hips, I snuck a little closer, and my feelings for Skye settled deeper and deeper. I'd had a crush on her for years. Feeling drawn to her was how I ended up befriending her and led to us becoming best friends. As the years passed, it only got stronger.

But now, touching her, the romantic song, her body so close to mine, something clicked into place deep inside me.

When she turned her head up to look at me, I stepped close, pressed my body to hers, and moved my right hand to the nape of her neck. She had her shiny brown hair up in a complicated twist, leaving her shoulders and neck bare. Only two spaghetti straps held her pink tank top up, something I'd thanked my lucky stars for when she'd walked in.

"Anthony," she whispered. Her plump lips parted slightly, drawing my gaze until all I could see or hear or smell was Skye. Her soft mouth. Her breathy voice.

I moved my face closer to hers and inhaled her scent, vanilla and something fruity. Citrus, maybe. She curved her neck, accepting my advance. The sound of her pulse ricocheted in my ears.

My heart pounded in my chest and my dragon roared his happiness that we were going to kiss Skye, finally. I hadn't shifted yet, but I'd always been connected to my dragon. Only our witch's blessings kept us from shifting as children, which could be traumatic for anyone who might happen upon a toddler shifting into a small, vicious little dragon.

As soon as my lips touched hers, a burning sensation began on my arm. I knew what it was but ignored it in favor of continuing the kiss. I didn't push it with my tongue or anything. I wasn't sure how many guys Skye had kissed in her life, but I didn't want to freak her out now, this first time I got to taste her.

The burn on my arm intensified and I pulled back, biting back a hiss of pain. Pulling Skye into my arms, I hugged her close and continued to sway, giving me a chance to look at my arm over her shoulder. Sure enough, on my inner right forearm, the faintest outline of the fated mate tattoo had begun to form.

I grinned down at the mark, which would be invisible to humans, but the other dragons would be able to see it once it came in darker or if they looked closely. I swayed, absolutely stunned by this new development.

Skye shifted in my arms, sliding her hands up my back and resting her head on my shoulder. Her movement pulled me out of my astonishment enough to realize the other dragons in the room had picked up on my change in energy. They were all stiff, looking around as if for a sound only they could hear. If they didn't chill, all the humans would notice their identical behavior. They were anxious, unsure what this energy was.

Shit. It was me, and it was good, but they didn't know that. I wasn't alpha yet, so the connection wasn't the same. If I'd already been alpha, they would've known that I was experiencing a happy event.

Skye pulled back and looked up at me. "Are you okay?" she asked. Something caught her eye, and she looked around the room. "What's going on?"

I gaped at her silently, without the first damn clue how to answer her. "I've got to go," I whispered. "Sorry."

Panic bloomed in my chest. If I didn't get my emotions under control, the clan was going to move into defense mode. This was something I'd trained against, but seeing my mate mark had broken through all my defenses. As the alpha heir, I had to control my emotions. It would be even more paramount as alpha, but at least then they would've known what was going on without me having to call a meeting or something stupid like that.

Darting toward the kitchen, around the corner from where I'd found Skye, and down a long hall, I sighed in relief when I spotted my mom and made a beeline for her. "What's going on?" she hissed when she saw my face.

I opened my mouth to explain, but she grabbed my hand and yanked me toward her. "Oh, honey." Her voice was overjoyed. "Mitch!" she called.

My dad appeared from behind her. He'd probably been bugging the caterers in the kitchen, sneaking extra sweets. And Mom had likely been on her way to catch him doing it.

"What's wrong?" Dad asked. "I sensed the pack getting upset."

"Mitch, look." Mom tugged on my arm, nearly knocking me off balance.

When Dad saw the glow, which had begun to brighten, his face broke into a wide grin. "My boy! Who is it?" He was delighted to see I'd found my fated mate.

He wasn't going to be delighted for long. "It's Skylar," I said in a low voice after looking around to make sure we were alone in the hallway.

Both of my parents' faces paled as the implications of the name I'd said sunk in.

"A human?" My mother dropped my arm and recoiled. "That can't be."

"It's not possible, son." Dad put his hand on my shoulder. "Maybe you were near Skylar when it happened, but it has to be someone else."

I gave him a flat look. "Give me more credit than that, Dad. I know who these feelings and emotions are for. I've known for a long time, but I…" It was hard to say this stuff to my parents.

"What?" Dad asked. "You what?"

"I kissed her," I said in the quietest whisper I could manage. "That's when the burn started."

Dad's eyebrows settled into an angry line. "Dragons don't mate with humans," he said in a growly, deep voice.

I wasn't taking it, though. "Obviously, they can," I hissed and shoved my forearm under his nose. "Or this is just a figment of my imagination, I guess?"

What happened next changed the course of the rest of my life. Dad dropped his voice deeper, going into his alpha register. When he gave a command with that voice, nobody in his clan could refuse him. "You will go tell your friends the party is over. Invent whatever excuse you want to. You've got until the end of the week to say goodbye. You're going away."

I couldn't argue, however many retorts sprang to mind. I'd never been so angry in my life, and no doubt the entire clan was close to losing it out in the party thanks to my father's emotions and now my anger.

Fate chose Skye for me, but my father was so prejudiced against humans that he wouldn't even consider that.

"Go, send them away," he growled.

Biting back my retorts, I turned on my heel and walked into the party. "Sorry, everyone. Something has come up." I waved my right arm.

The tattoo had begun to glow enough that the entire clan could see it now. Humans never would be able to, such was the magic that made it, but all of the clan now knew why I was sending everyone away.

Tessa's face caught my eye. She looked overjoyed as she stared at my arm, still waving in the air. Her face had a glow of hopefulness on it. I'd suspected for a while that she had a crush on me. Now I was sure. That was going to be nothing but inconvenient, at best.

I got everyone out the door, shrugging at Skye as she went along with the crowd. "Call you later," I mouthed as she let herself get hurried out the door.

Everyone would probably think we were even worse of a cult now that I'd ended my party like this. It would've been better all along to just have had the party with the clan.

***

I'd put it off as long as I could. She'd been texting and calling me, but I'd sent excuse after excuse not to see her. Now my bags were packed, and with my dad being all alpha-hole, I had no choices left.

"Hey." I scuffed my toe as she walked up and stood close. For a second, she seemed like she wanted to give me a hug, but I firmly kept my hands in my jeans pockets to discourage her from touching me. "Thanks for meeting me."

My dragon retreated deep inside me, sullen and confused about why we couldn't be with Skye. He was part of me, and I of him. It wasn't like he could talk to me or vice versa, but sometimes his emotions overpowered me.

Like now. I wanted to cry and wrap my arms around Skye, proclaiming my love for her and promising never to leave her.

But that wasn't going to happen. Even if I'd tried, the alpha commands on me prevented it. My dad was being a total douchebag about it, which was so unlike him. I didn't know what the hell to think.

"Of course." Skye touched my arm. "What is going on?"

I blurted out the lie we'd come up with. It sounded wooden and rote even to my ears, but I pushed forward with it anyway. "I got a scholarship to a prestigious boarding school in England. My parents are making me go."

Skye snorted. "Your parents are loaded. What do you need with a scholarship?"

I looked around the park, trying to think of what to say. "Did I say scholarship? I meant I got admitted and they didn't think I would. It will really help me get into a good college and medical school, so they're putting their foot down about it."

Skye's face went from amused and disbelieving to confused and a little angry. "Okay, so England. We can video chat, and you'll be home in like two years to go to college. Maybe we can work on going to the same one."

Leave it to her to try to be optimistic. We'd been best friends for so long, she couldn't conceive the rest of our lives apart.

Well, neither could I. Especially with the burning that was still on my right forearm, which worsened now that we were together.

"Sure, yeah," I said, but we both knew I was lying.

Skye's eyes registered betrayal as she recoiled. "So, that's just it?" I watched her chest rise and fall as she tried to hide her upset.

I pretended I couldn't hear her heart beating out of her chest, and backed away. "I'll see you around, Skye."

I had to get away from her. Her pain spurred my own and I barely made it back to my family's land before I shifted, my dragon taking the reins and launching us into the air. Once upon a time, shifting was painful for dragons, but painless shifts was another byproduct of having a clan witch. She spelled each of us once a year to have painless shifts. What would we do without Sammy?

My parents were somewhere nearby, flying. We were able to communicate telepathically, and I couldn't stop myself. *I'll never forgive you.*

I tried not to think about how much I hated them, but it came through anyway because, within a few seconds, awareness of them disappeared from my mind. They'd

shifted back, probably unable to stand feeling my pain.

Good. I hoped it haunted them.

Chapter 1 - Skylar

Eighteen Years Later

"Put that under your pillow." I handed the teddy bear to my patient. Kendrick was eight and about to have his appendix out. "If you get scared, tell the teddy. He'll keep your secret." The little guy was nervous, but his big brother was out in the hall, waiting for me to finish my presurgery exam. I was fairly sure Kendrick was too worried about his big brother thinking he was a sissy to be honest about how terrified he was about the surgery.

Kendrick grinned at me with a couple of missing teeth. "Thanks, Nurse Skye."

I winked at him and went into the hall, typing the info into my tablet. It would notify the surgeon that I'd completed the forms needed, and his mother had signed everything.

"That's it for me." I plopped the tablet down on the charging station and plugged it in. "All the paperwork is caught up, and I'm going to lunch."

The ward clerk gave me an amused look. "So eager to escape the floor?"

Laughing, I held up my hands. "Of course not. But I *am* starving." Normally, I worked in the primary care clinic on the other side of the hospital. When the peds floor had requested an extra half-shift so their head nurse could go to yearly sexual harassment training, I'd volunteered.

Why not? I had nothing better to do, and I loved my job. After telling the rest of the team goodbye, I headed to the cafeteria. There was a cafe on my side of the hospital, and I almost always stopped there. Today, I'd come to the cafeteria on this side. Someone had mentioned they had taco salad, which I loved.

Unfortunately, I didn't see anyone I knew, so I grabbed a small booth and played a game on my phone while I ate. This was preferable to going home and cooking for one.

A woman's voice behind me had my ears prickling. "Have you seen him yet?"

I didn't mean to listen in, but they were in the booth directly behind mine. I couldn't help it.

"No," a new voice said. "But I heard he's gorgeous."

I took a big bite of my taco salad and tried to mind my own business. It wasn't easy.

"Dr. White had to go on emergency leave this morning, and…" Someone dropped a tray nearby and I missed the new doctor's name. "He was already in town and had applied at the hospital, so he got brought on immediately."

"What's wrong with Dr. White?" the second voice asked.

"His mom fell and broke her hip. He's going to take some time off to take care of her. Must be nice to be able to do that. When it happened to my Nana, we had to put her in a state-funded home."

She sounded a little bitter, but I didn't blame her. I would've been in her shoes, too. But I never had a Nana, so what did I know?

"He used to live in Bluewater, apparently, and decided to move back home. That's all I got from the nurse that scrubbed in with him on surgery this morning."

So, the new doctor was a surgeon. That was fine. It meant my schedule wouldn't change. Dr. White worked in the primary care clinic a lot but wasn't a surgeon. I wondered how they'd revamp the duties to make it all work, but that was way above my paygrade.

I wondered if I'd known him before. We'd had several doctors come and go from Bluewater Memorial since I started here long ago as a CNA. It was probably one of them. I couldn't think of a single one that I had any issues with, so whoever it was would be fine.

I'd intended to go straight home, but as I passed my dad's body shop, I decided to pull in at the last second. My shift had ended at five, but he kept the shop open until at least seven. I knew he'd be there, working away.

"Dad?" I called as I walked into the bay. "You working?"

"Hey, sugar!" Dad popped his head out from under an old truck. "It's about time you stopped by to see me."

"Yeah, snookums, where've you been?" My dad's right-hand man, Cooter, walked in from the office. "Working yourself to death?"

Dad looked at me with his eyebrows raised. "He's not wrong."

I rolled my eyes and walked over to the toolbox beside the truck. "Says the man who will probably be here banging on these cars until it's dark."

He rolled back underneath the truck. "Hand me the ten!"

I snorted and got the socket for him. "Sure, sure." I'd been handing him tools since I could walk.

"How's work?" he asked over the clanks of whatever he was doing with the socket I'd handed him.

"Fine. Nothing new. There's some new doctor I haven't met yet." I leaned against the truck and about five seconds later jerked upright when Dad smacked my leg. "Sorry!"

I knew better than to lean against vehicles while they were jacked up.

"What's in your head?" He rolled out from under the truck and sat up, handing me the tool to put away.

I shrugged. "I just wasn't thinking, is all."

Cooter snorted. "You look like you've got a bug up your butt."

I shot Cooter a glare and pointed at him. "*You* hush."

He glared right back. "*You* need a life."

"Hey," I said defensively. "I have a life."

Dad had to chime in, too. "A life outside work."

Oh. Yeah. Maybe.

"You're going to end up like me, working until you exhaust yourself before falling into bed and getting up the next day to do it all again."

I didn't tell him I'd already been doing that. It wasn't like I had a lot of friends to go out with or a boyfriend or anything.

"It's fine. It's not like I want to be a grandfather one day or anything." Oh, great. He was bringing out the big guns. "I mean, you're my only daughter. I guess I could always sign up for one of those programs where kids come to visit the elderly."

I dropped my hands beside me and threw my head back. "Dad." He was laying it on thick. If he said one more thing about it, I was going to end up biting his head off.

"Oh, you know I'm not serious, sugar. I'm happy if you're happy."

"Yeah, yeah." I smiled at him until he rolled himself back under the truck. He never had put pressure on me like that. If, one day, he died without grandkids, he'd never make me feel bad about it.

I would, though. I'd never told him about my PCOS. Somehow, I just never could bring myself to. How could I tell him that he'd never have grandchildren? I supposed that wasn't true though, I still could adopt. I'd been feeling the biological tick. Not to get pregnant, necessarily, but to decide one way or the other. I didn't even know if I'd make a good mother. I'd never had one myself, how would I know if mothering would come easily to me? And I wasn't sure if I wanted to give up my independence, such as it was. I mean, I didn't go out often, but when I did, I called up my best friend, Kaylee, and we went out. Or stayed in, depending on our mood.

But oh, what joy I saw on my patients' faces when they held their little babies in their arms. And goodness knew I'd tried to get pregnant, for a long time. I'd been hoping it was Bret that was firing blanks and not my PCOS, up until he got his side chick pregnant.

"Dad," I called under the truck. "What are your dinner plans?"

"Cooter made chili," he yelled back. He'd slid quite far underneath.

Cooter's chili was pretty damn good. I turned to find the older man grinning at me with a knowing look on his face. Dad and Cooter had been best friends all my life. When I was younger, I'd called him Uncle Cooter. "Save me some?" I asked.

He rolled his eyes and looked down at the table full

of tools in front of him. I followed his glance to find a

grocery store bag on the side of the table closest to me.

Cocking my head, I gave him a sly smile. "Uncle C,

is that what I think it is?"

"If you think it's a baggie of corn chips and a

baggie of cheese and a baggie of sour cream plus a big

bowl of chili, then you're as smart as I think you are."

I squealed, playing it up a little, because I knew

how happy it made Cooter. This was how he showed love

to me, Dad, and the other guys in the shop. He cooked for

us all the time. He wasn't quick with the words of

affection, but he made a damn good roast.

He was covered in oil and grime, so I didn't hug

him, but I did give him a huge grin. "Thanks. I'll take it to

work with me tomorrow."

He nodded. "Good. Get out of here."

Dad rolled out from under the truck again and stood. "We don't like you driving at night."

I shook my head at both of them. "You're worse than a couple of old hens."

Dad shot Cooter a glare. "Maybe he is."

I waved at them and left them arguing. They'd be arguing until they were old and frail. Hopefully, anyway. If something happened to one of them, I wasn't sure what the other would do. They'd been working together for so long, they were like a staple in our small town. Everyone came to Will's to get their cars fixed. And everyone thought Dad's name was Will and called him that. Only people who knew me knew that our last name was Wills, and Dad had used it in a bit of word play for the shop name.

When I turned on my car, I used the fancy-schmancy voice feature to call my best friend on the way home. "Call Kaylee," I said in a clear, firm voice.

"Hey, biatch!" Kaylee always answered with some inappropriate phrase or another. "What's going on?"

"Should I have kids out of obligation?" I blurted. Kaylee was the sort to lay it all out there with.

She burst out laughing. "Leave it to you. You know the answer to that."

I sighed and turned on my blinker to head away from town and Dad's shop. "I know." I wasn't trying to sound sullen, but that's how it came out.

"What's brought this on?" A thumping sound came through the car's stereo speakers and when her voice came back on, it was apparent she'd put me on speaker. "Why all the sudden interest in having obligatory babies?"

"I don't know. Dad said something about wanting grandkids one day." The light turned green, and I turned onto the coastal road that led to my small cottage home.

"Then tell him to buy one." Kaylee's flat voice made me laugh, as I'd known it would. "Or he can have another kid, if he wants to try again for a boy."

We both laughed, her more sarcastically than me. There was a tinge of hurt in my laughter, because I was convinced that he'd really wanted a boy all along.

"Listen, if it's meant for you to have a baby, you will. It'll happen. And in the meantime, we can get drunk and flirt with sexy men."

"Or in your case, take them home and help them lose their innocence." I grinned out at the road as Kaylee laughed harder.

"You're thinking about Bret, aren't you?" she asked once she'd calmed her giggles.

I sighed. "Well, I wasn't, until you brought him up."

"You're a terrible liar. Have you seen him lately?"

It was impossible to work at the hospital and not see him. He was half the reason I usually went to the cafe and not the cafeteria. He liked the full service of the cafeteria and went there most often for his lunches.

"I don't care about Bret or his life, or his new baby mama."

"The offer to burn his house down stands."

Bret had been my college boyfriend, and then fiancé. We'd lived together in a large apartment near the hospital in downtown Bluewater Cove. The wedding date had come and gone this past winter while Bret was at our apartment with his new fiancé and her pregnant belly. He'd been cheating on me all along, apparently, and it only came to light when his current squeeze got pregnant. He'd then tried to blame me by saying I was too busy and worked too many hours.

He was lonely.

"And I still might take you up on it, but honestly, Kaylee, the hurt isn't nearly as bad as it used to be. And me thinking about babies might have been spurred a little by them, but it's a valid question. At my age, don't I have the right to be wondering if it's time to get pregnant?" I'd be turning thirty-five soon, and that was considered a geriatric pregnancy and came with its own set of complications.

"Yes, you have the right to think about it. As long as you're not obsessing over that dirtbag."

"I know that his cheating was his problem, not mine. It wasn't my fault." She'd been drilling it into my head since it happened, and somewhere along the way, the reality that it *had* been Bret's fault and not mine had sunk in and I'd finally begun to believe it.

"I'm glad to hear it. Now, when are you off again?"

I'd picked up a few shifts. "I'm honestly not sure. Let me check and I'll text you. Girls' night?"

"Hell, yes."

We hung up as I pulled into the driveway of my new cottage. When I moved out of Bret's, I'd moved back in with Dad in his place behind the auto shop for a little while, but then decided I wanted some time to myself. I'd gone from Dad's to the dorm room, where I roomed with Kaylee. Not that I regretted that, she'd become a lifelong friend. After the dorm, I'd moved in with Bret, then when that went to hell, back to Dad's.

For the last six months, I'd lived in my cottage, alone.

And it was wonderful. If I wanted to eat ice cream in bed, naked, I did. If I wanted to dance off the ice cream I'd eaten in bed, I did that, too. I watched TV if I wanted to, cleaned when I wanted to and had my girly face products and lingerie spread out all over the house.

The only thing that sucked was eating. Cooking for one was a major bummer. I avoided it, generally, eating at the hospital or Dad's whenever I could. Eating out so much meant that I danced more than I used to, but that was okay, too. There was nothing wrong with streaming exercise videos to earn the large fries instead of small.

After a shower, I made the bed and curled up in it, throwing my robe at the end and enjoying the feel of the clean sheets on my naked, damp body.

I considered myself, trying to be as self-aware as I could. I wasn't ugly, though I also wouldn't have said I was the hottest person in Bluewater. Sometimes I was funny, and I was loyal for sure. I didn't steal or anything. Dad had installed a pretty decent moral compass.

My teeth were always clean, and I'd never suffered from acne. In short, I was decent.

So why did men seem repulsed by me? Bret was the only man that had ever shown me any attention, and I'd fallen for him hook, line, and sinker. He'd kept me at home as his steady, boring wife-to-be while he'd snuck around with all the exciting women he'd wanted to.

The only other man I'd ever had any sort of relationship with sprang to mind. Anthony Mason. He'd been my best friend all through my childhood and half of high school. He'd kissed me one time, then disappeared, saying his family had gotten him into some prestigious school in England.

Except that he'd never sent so much as an email. He'd said we would video chat or text, and though I'd sent a few messages, I'd quickly given up when there was no reply.

That hadn't stopped me from stalking his social media. When he left, social media was just getting a real foothold and we'd both just made accounts on the two biggest platforms. He'd never unfriended me, but I was always very careful about how much I let him see and I never, ever liked, commented, or reacted to any of his posts.

It was petty, but it was life. And he seemed to be living his best life, by the looks of his accounts.

He'd left me as if I'd never mattered to him in the least. No way would I let him know I stalked him occasionally online.

I fell asleep thinking about him, and when my alarm went off the next morning, I woke with a dream slipping away so fast I had no idea what it had been about, but somehow, I knew, just *knew* it was the recurring dream I had where Anthony kissed me and as soon as our lips touched, he jerked back and looked down at me as if I repulsed him.

As soon as I walked into the primary care clinic, the receptionist, Cam, skittered across the office. "Come on," she said. "You're late." Her layers of bracelets clacked as she moved.

"Sorry, I stopped for coffee. I was out." I held up my large to-go cup as proof.

"That's all well and good, but we're meeting the new doctor. He's replacing Dr. White for the foreseeable future."

She grabbed my arm as soon as I stashed my purse and jacket in the back room. "Hurry," Camilla urged.

We walked into the staff room, the last ones to enter. They'd left the chairs closest to the door open around the big conference table. We sat and looked at the head of the table to find the hospital CEO standing with the new doctor.

"Thanks everyone for taking the time to have this little introductory meeting," he said.

I looked at the new doctor standing beside him for the first time to discover his gaze was glued to me.

My jaw dropped as I tried not to shit a brick.

It was Anthony fucking Mason.

Chapter 2 - Anthony

The old tattoo had tingled once yesterday, but I'd expected that. I'd only been back in town for a few days. When the time came for me to come back to Bluewater, my parents had warned me that Skylar hadn't moved away, as I had always hoped she would. I was prepared to run into her again and do my best to ignore the mating call.

Yeah, right. I should've stayed gone. I'd never intended to come back and take over as alpha during Skylar's lifetime, but my father up and decided he wanted to retire and enjoy the good life, so he said. Then, in the next breath, he told me I couldn't get any ideas about Skylar, that humans and dragons couldn't mate.

I should've told him no. Told him to wait.

But here I was, getting ready to be introduced to my new team, and my tattoo tingled again. It had been tingling for two or three minutes now. She had to have entered the building, at least.

They'd warned me Skylar was a nurse, but I'd stopped them there. I didn't want to know. As my tattoo flared to life, scalding my arm for the first time since I was sixteen years old, I stiffened and looked at the door of the small conference room.

And she walked in. She didn't notice me, either. My dragon roared inside me, urging me to make my presence known, but all I could do was stand there and try not to look shocked by her presence.

I schooled my features into an inscrutable mask, something I'd perfected during my intern years. And finally, after what felt like a dozen lifetimes, she looked up and met my gaze. My breath caught in my throat. My tattoo burned until it throbbed to the beat of my heart, which was beating in double time.

After all these years of my instincts screaming at me to go home and find Skye, there she was, sitting at a conference table in front of me.

I knew I should've checked to make sure she didn't work here. Of *course* she worked at this hospital. Of all the doctor's offices and all the hospitals in the world, she worked here. She could've gotten a job at a nursing home, pediatrician's office, telehealth, even.

But no. She worked at the one place I wanted to work now that I'd be in Bluewater indefinitely. As of the next new moon, I couldn't move away from the cove without moving the entire clan with me.

They'd go if I ordered it. But I'd never do that to them. This was their home, our home, and had been for a couple of centuries now, though the clan had grown exponentially in the last hundred years or so. So much that the townsfolk had decided years ago we were some weird cult.

I had no idea how to remedy that situation. I didn't even know what to do about my fated freaking mate sitting right in front of me, pretending she didn't know me.

Starting something up with Skye would mean directly disobeying my alpha. But he wouldn't be alpha for long. Soon, it would be me. That changed things a lot.

Focusing on the job, I tried my damndest to pretend the love of my life wasn't sitting in front of me, her shiny brown hair still full of red highlights. If I breathed deep, I would've been able to smell her. I had no idea what *that* would do to my blazing arm.

Focusing on work was easy, but ignoring my arm wasn't. I rubbed it self-consciously as I introduced myself. "Hello, everyone. I'm really looking forward to being back home and working in the town I grew up in. I can't wait to get to know all of you." I smiled encouragingly, meeting everyone's gaze—except Skye's. Her, I glanced over. If I looked again, I was liable to ask her to excuse herself and come talk to me in the hall. After all these years, seeing her again was like a ray of sunshine warming my face…and burning my arm.

Sucking in a deep breath against the pain, I continued introducing myself. "As I said, I grew up here and went to Bluewater High until my junior year. Then, I was accepted to the Regents' School for the Gifted in London, where I finished my junior and senior years. After that, I attended Harvard University, then Harvard Medical School. I accepted a position at Boston General until a family matter brought me back here."

I hadn't said it to impress anyone, though if I managed to impress Skye in the process, I wouldn't have been upset. I'd dated a few shifter women over the years, but my dragon and I had known what we were missing. Though the pain on the mark had faded the farther away I got from Skye, nothing was ever the same after kissing her. "So, that's me. I hope to get to know all of you very soon."

The hospital CEO, Dr. Smith, beamed at the table. "Why don't you all tell Dr. Mason your names and specialties, at least, before we go face the day?" He looked at his wristwatch. "We just have enough time."

Looking to his right, he pointed at the woman who had walked in with Skye. I tried to pay attention to her, but my gaze kept slipping to her left, to Skye.

"I'm Camilla. Just Cam." I forced myself to listen and look at her. I was overwhelmed with being in the same room as my mate again, but that didn't mean I could ignore these other people. I'd be working with them day in and day out. "I'm the primary care office manager, and the only full-time receptionist, though we have several part-timers."

I nodded at her and smiled, then counted to three before looking at Skye. She narrowed her eyes at me.

What was I supposed to say? Anything? I hadn't said anything to Cam. Panic scratched at my throat.

When I was about to open my mouth and say her name, Skye spoke. "My name is Skylar Wills, APRN, CPNP-PC, FAANP, FAAN. I'm the only nurse practitioner in primary care, so I float out of peds frequently." She arched one eyebrow, challenging me. I ducked my head and smiled. She'd get no challenge from me. I was impressed by her credentials.

As I continued down the table, missing everyone's names and references completely, I thought about what she'd said. By the letters she'd rattled off after her name, I knew she was a nurse practitioner with the pediatric specialty and likely had a master's degree in nursing. She was a fellow of the prestigious American Association of

Nurse Practitioners as well as a fellow of the American Association of Nurses.

Most everyone else just rattled off if they were a nurse or LPN, and so on. Only Skye went so far as to list everything. She knew exactly who I was and wanted me to know that she saw me. I couldn't help but wonder if in all that time, all that schooling had kept her too distracted to find a long-term boyfriend. Or even worse, husband. I didn't see a ring.

Damn it, she was so hot. She'd always been intelligent, but I'd never known she wanted to go into nursing. I'd stalked her on social media nearly every day since I joined and *friended* her on there, but she rarely posted. I didn't know much more about her from her social media than I'd gotten via hearsay from my family and clanmates that had lived in the town this whole time.

My tattoo kept burning, distracting me not only from the people around the table but it even flared hard enough to distract me from Skye herself.

Dr. Smith dismissed the room, but I didn't move. It was probably rude of me, but all I could do was stare at Skylar.

And she stared back. And she didn't move. We kept our gazes on one another until the room emptied. I finally looked away to see her friend, Cam, give her and me a strange look before backing slowly out of the room and closing the door behind her. "Okay, then," she whispered in the hall right before the door closed.

"Why are you here?" Her voice was flat and the furthest thing from welcoming I could've imagined. "Or am I hallucinating?"

I shook my head. "I'm here. And I was telling the truth. My mom and dad asked me to move back home."

Different emotions passed over her face until she squashed them all down and settled on anger. I couldn't blame her for the insincerity in her voice as she stood. "Well, so nice to have you back. I look forward to working with you." She didn't mean it. "It's good to know you're alive and breathing and I can see it in person instead of stalking you occasionally on social media." That she meant.

At least I wasn't the only one doing the stalking, but damn. I felt like shit, if a little smug that I wasn't the only one creeping social media. I knew my reasons for staying away, and a part of me had hoped she'd missed me as much as I'd missed her. But the bigger part had hoped she'd forget me. I wanted to know she wasn't hurt because of me.

"If that's all, *Dr.* Mason?"

My hopes fell through the floor. She hated me. I nodded and watched her walk out of the conference room.

Dr. Smith came in the moment she left. "One moment, Ms. Wills."

She stalked back into the room, but Dr. Smith was totally oblivious. "I'll leave it to Ms. Wills here to show you the ropes. I know you were happy with the schedule Dr. White left, yes?"

I didn't remember discussing that whatsoever. It must've been one of the things I missed during the staff meeting, so I just smiled and nodded.

"Good, good." He looked at Skye. "You'll show him around and baby him a bit until he's broken in?"

She gritted her teeth but nodded. Dr. Smith didn't notice a thing. "Good, good. Good. I'll leave you to it!"

With a sigh, Skye watched him walk out. "Come on," she said sullenly. "We've already got patients."

"I know how important routine is," I said and hurried around the table to join her. "I'll do my best to keep to it. I don't want to throw anyone off."

"What's your deal with surgeries?" she asked over her shoulder as she hurried down the hallway. I wanted to talk more, but it looked like we were going to get right to work. She led me to a nurses' station. This clinic was set up much like a hospital floor, which I wasn't used to.

Well, I was used to working in a hospital, not a primary care clinic. But the position that had opened up had been for primary care in peds, not surgery. "I'm a pediatric surgeon," I said. "But I'll only be doing surgeries as my schedule allows, hopefully, enough to keep me from getting rusty. As of right now, I'm a primary care doctor."

She gave me a glowering look. "I see." Reaching over the counter, she pulled out a small tablet. "Here is our chart. It's all digital now. You need to plug them in between each patient, or you run the risk of them going dead. If we have a power failure, we've got only the batteries on these tablets and the backup generator in the server room to print off what records we need to go back to analog."

I nodded. Many hospitals were moving to similar systems with the speed technology had been advancing just since I got out of medical school. It was digitize or get left behind.

"May I?" I asked.

Skye handed the tablet over without a word.

I was relieved to see a program I was familiar with. "We used this at Harvard, during medical school, to run simulations."

She gave me a tight, angry smile, her green eyes flashing. "I'm sorry we're not as advanced as the hospital you worked for in Boston."

"No, you misunderstand me." I opened the file for the first patient on the schedule. A six-year-old boy complaining of a sore throat. After skimming his history and other intake questions, I gave the tablet back to Skye. "Boston was the one that was behind. For them to be as advanced as they are, cutting edge, really, they desperately need to upgrade their basic record-keeping systems. Harvard was always using the latest and greatest to try to train the doctors in the newest methods, including the newest software." I rattled on, desperate for her to not think I was insulting little Bluewater Memorial. "I love this hospital. I meant that."

I'd wanted to move home from the moment I completed my residency and had even looked into *doing* my residency here at Bluewater. I figured I'd commute in so I wouldn't actually live in the county, and not disobey my alpha. It would've been on a technicality, but still.

She sighed. "Come on. The RN should be ready for you to go in."

Nodding, I followed her to the first room. The layout of the offices was a little labyrinth-like, but I knew I'd get the hang of it soon enough. Skye stopped at a door. "This one is yours; I'll take the next one down. If I go in with you on each patient, we'll get hopelessly behind."

Nodding, I took the tablet again. "I've done this a time or two. I gotcha."

After examining the patient, I asked the RN to order a strep test and went out to the hall to the little alcove set up for doctors to put their notes in before going to the next room. It helped us be able to see more patients each day without getting way behind on our notes.

As soon as I put in the info I needed, I checked the schedule, then looked at the intake notes, and I noticed some problems. The nurses weren't filling the notes out completely and hadn't updated each section.

That was a problem. I'd actually had cases before where the most obscure fact about the family history or patient symptoms had helped diagnose. If they didn't fill it in completely every time, something might get missed.

In most parts of my life, I wasn't a stickler about much of anything. Except charting. I had to be a dick about it, whether I wanted to be or not.

Skye walked out of the room beside the one I'd seen my first patient in. "Hey," I said. "Can I ask you something?"

She nodded as she tapped at her tablet. "What's up, doctor?"

"First, please, call me Anthony. Or Tony."

Skylar sighed and looked up from her tablet as if I'd asked her to do me some huge favor. "I think it's best if we keep things professional, Dr. Mason."

Fine. I'd play along for now. "Well, what would you recommend for getting the nurses to chart a little more thoroughly?"

She narrowed her eyes. "What's wrong with the way we chart?" She'd lumped herself in with the rest of the nurses, though she was more doctor than a nurse, despite not having an MD or PhD.

"It needs to be more thorough. I'll play along and work whatever schedule, and I will be as flexible as I can. Easier for me to blend in here than for the entire staff to adapt to my way of doing things. But one thing I can't bend on is charting."

Her nostrils flared. "We're thorough. But I'll make sure the staff knows to dot every I and cross every T. Will that be sufficient?"

I sighed, but what could I do? "Thank you, Ms. Wills."

"You'll have no problems with us." She looked at her tablet again. "If you'll excuse me, we both have more patients. They'll all be in these rooms along these halls, and the patient portal on your tablet will tell you if they're ready for you to go in and in what order."

I nodded but didn't remind her I was familiar with the program. She knew. Skylar walked down the hall and into one of the rooms. I tracked her with my hearing and an innate sense that I'd never had with anyone else. I was pretty sure as long as my arm was burning, I'd be able to find her anywhere in the hospital.

"How do you know Dr. Mason?" a female voice asked her. I was fairly sure it was Cam, from the meeting.

"I don't know him. Not anymore." Her words hurt. But she wasn't wrong. She didn't know me. We hadn't seen each other in eighteen years or so. But I had every damn intention of fixing it. I'd had to wait until I became alpha, but that was happening at the next full moon.

The day wore on and every time Skylar and I passed one another in the halls, nothing got better. She was just this side of openly hostile with me.

When she talked to the patients or the other staff, it was with a kind, gentle voice. With me, it was the utmost of professionalism.

My old NP back in Boston called it professional bitch, but heaven help me, I never would've said that to Skye's face. Or her back. Or ever uttered the words out loud.

By the end of the day, I knew I had my work cut out for me. The tension between Skye and me was thick enough to cut. I had to fight against my parents for this relationship, and now I was going to have to fight Skylar, for, well…for herself. It was time for me to stop this farce and claim my mate.

Chapter 3 - Skylar

Finally, it was Friday. TGIF. I used to watch special shows on TV on Fridays, and ever since, it was ingrained in me to look forward to the weekend. Every week, though, it never failed, I got behind on paperwork. I had to stay behind and catch up because going in on a Monday and facing paperwork from the week before was never a good thing. I'd learned that very early on. Always finish it on Friday.

I finally finished and headed for the front. As soon as I came out of the back hallway, I saw Cam, still at the desk, working on paperwork of her own. Half the time she was there later than me, updating billing records and the like. Since we'd put her on salary, she just did it, no matter how often I tried to get her to hire someone part-time. "It's not in the budget," was her rote answer.

"I'm sorry, dear, but the doctors have all gone," she said. I stepped forward and peered around the corner to see a tired-looking mom and the top of a blonde-headed child's head on the other side of the counter.

With an internal sigh, I walked closer until I could see the child. Strep was going around severely, and the ER was probably a cluster right now.

The mom spotted me. "Can you see us?" she asked pitifully. "She's running a fever, and now I'm not feeling so great."

"I could see you," I said. "But hospital policy requires there be a doctor and a nurse present. I could be either in this situation, but I'm the only one here." I hated to tell her that, knowing something nonemergent like this would take ages at the ER.

"I'm here." Damn it. Anthony's voice was the last one I wanted to hear. Why couldn't it have been one of my nurses? It'd been a trying week. Working in close proximity with Anthony after not being around him for so long was beyond strange. It was like I didn't know how to act around him anymore. He was a different person. The guy I'd known and loved was a young boy, but Dr. Mason was a grown-ass man. His voice was deeper. He'd grown even taller and though I tried so hard to ignore it, he was a *lot* more handsome. He'd outgrown every bit of gawky teen that my best friend had been back then.

On top of that, it was odd seeing him in his element. He was obviously a good doctor and loved his chosen career. The kids all loved him, too.

Not to mention the moms. It hadn't escaped my notice that suddenly there were fewer dads bringing their kids in for their checkups. How those mothers had gotten the word in one week, I had no idea.

Another thing that I hadn't missed was the fact that we both chose careers in the medical field *and* we both chose to work with children. Again, I ignored it because it didn't matter or mean anything. Not at all. Not even a little. Who cared what field he'd gone into? Not me.

"Great," I chirped. "Come on, you guys. Cam will get you checked in." I shot her a grateful look before turning around and going back toward the exam rooms. I waited there for Cam to finish, staunchly ignoring Dr. Mason, who waited beside me, then the mom and daughter walked into the back waiting area. "Come on, you get no-wait service."

The mom beamed at me. "I'm Briana. And I can't thank you enough."

Waving her off, I grabbed a tablet and started the questions.

Dr. Mason had requested that the information be filled in completely, so as we walked to the closest exam room, I made sure to be thorough, not skipping the least little question, no matter that I knew damn well this child had strep and all we needed to do was the test, which was easy as pie. They even made strep tests that could be done at home. No medical degree required, though most adults didn't realize they could get them.

Fifteen minutes later, after I went through every possible question and family history section, I swabbed the sweet girl's throat. "Okay, Hayden, this will be uncomfortable for a second."

Dr. Mason stood in the background, basically useless. But I hadn't needed his help, anyway, just the stupid policy that there had to be two of us here. "Now, we just wait for this to react in the fluid, and we'll get you out of here."

"Thank you again, so much." Briana shot Dr. Mason a look, half interested and half curious why he was even there. I hadn't let him get a word in edgewise.

Sure enough, it was strep. I calculated the dosage for the antibiotic and wrote out a prescription for Hayden. "Here you go. There's a twenty-four-hour pharmacy across the street." Then, I looked up the ibuprofen dosage for Hayden's age and weight and wrote it down for her mother. It was super important to be careful with how much ibuprofen they got at that young age. "If she gets any worse, call us and come back in."

"I will. I just can't thank you enough. I'm a teacher, and my mom keeps Hayden after school. She'd told me she was feeling rough, but I didn't know how sick she was until far too late in the day when I picked her up."

"Hey, I get it. I'm glad we were still here."

"You and me both," Briana said. "Thanks again." She hesitated, and I waited a second. I'd been about to get up. "I hate to ask, but we're new in the area. Could you recommend anywhere a mom could, I don't know, unwind? My parents moved with us, so I have them constantly begging to babysit, but then I find myself at home alone and bored."

I grinned. "I get it. It's a small town, so you have to go seek out excitement. Let's see. There's Jace's Place downtown. It's a bar, mixed drinks and beer sort of place. Mostly they play music off a jukebox. It's a good place to shoot pool and throw darts. And right next door is the only club in town, Blue Cats. It's fun, but it can get too loud and overwhelming unless all you want to do is dance and drink."

Normally, I didn't get involved in any way with my patients or their families. But damn, this really was a teeny town. "Let me get your number," I said. She seemed really nice, anyway. Something about her made me want to give her a shot. "I'll text you and maybe show you around town one day soon?"

She beamed and rattled off her phone number, which I put in my phone. "Thanks. I'm glad I asked. I don't know how else to make friends, and I can't *only* be friends with the other teachers at my school. Besides, it seems like most of them are much older or much younger."

I chuckled. "We have that problem in this town. Like the whole town skipped a generation. Everyone is either in their forties or higher or twenties or lower."

We continued chatting as I walked her back before returning to clean the room. I got there to find Dr. Mason had already done it. He was putting the disinfectant up as I opened the door. "Well," I said, shocked. Doctors *never* cleaned rooms. "This might be a first for me."

He laughed and threw the paper towel away. "I'm not too good to wipe down an exam table."

Could've fooled me. "Thanks," I said brightly before whirling around to beat a hasty exit.

"Wait," he called.

Sighing, I froze. "Yeah?" I didn't even turn around to face him.

"I was glad to help, but we have schedules for a reason. I hope you'll follow protocol in the future, so my schedule isn't thrown off again."

I managed to keep my frustration in check, *barely*. I gritted my teeth and sucked in a deep breath, channeling every inch of professionalism I had in me. "I didn't mean to take up your *precious* time. I understand all too well that sometimes..." I turned to look at him over my shoulder, "you just have to run." I didn't miss his flinch before turning away, and I also didn't feel the least bit bad about it as I walked away. It might've been eighteen years ago, but he'd kissed me and then took off. The moment his lips met mine was literally the last time I'd laid eyes on him until that moment in the conference room.

With my head held high, I walked out of the office and grabbed my purse. Dr. Mason didn't follow.

What a dick.

Chapter 4 - Anthony

A coward. I was a damn coward. When my parents sent me to that school in London, I could've called. Sent a message. Hell, I could've written a letter. But contacting Skye would've meant defying my alpha.

And I was a coward who wouldn't defy my father. As my alpha, it would've been physically impossible for me to, anyway. I hadn't had a choice when I was sixteen. But what about when I was eighteen, about to go to Harvard? Or twenty-three, in medical school? Or twenty-nine, when I finished my residency? At that point, though I couldn't have defied a direct order from my alpha, I could've talked to my father and tried to come up with a better solution.

But I hadn't. And I hadn't come home. Not once. Now that I was thirty-four and had to come home, I realized how much I'd denied myself and my dragon.

The only good news I'd had this week was that I'd found out that Skye was single. Unattached. If I'd come back a year earlier, I would've found her in a relationship with a doctor at the hospital. An asshole, apparently.

Skylar's words stuck with me. They rang in my ears all night Friday, echoing when I woke Saturday morning. My running away from her had stuck with her, possibly as much as it had me. Had it thrown her entire life off-kilter as well? It certainly had mine.

I threw the blankets off with electricity running through me. It was the big day. The whole reason I came back to Bluewater Coast. I hadn't really expected to move straight into a position at the hospital, but the way it had worked out, I'd be taking over the clan the same night I was seeing them again for the first time since I left.

Much of my family and extended clan members had visited Boston at some point over the years, but I hadn't been with them as a group since my sixteenth birthday when everything went to Hell.

I was in store for a bunch of shit. Especially from the guys I hadn't seen in so long. I'd kept in better touch with them than Skylar, at least.

As the day wore on, I did my workout, neatened up around my bedroom in my parents' large home, and generally tried not to come out of my skin. By late afternoon, I couldn't stand it anymore.

"Mom, Dad," I called as I hurried down the stairs. "I'm going to go see Jace, calm down a bit before the ceremony. I'll see you tonight."

"Sure, honey. Your father is out flying, but I'll let him know." My mother was in the kitchen, likely making about ten times the amount of food we'd need for the big party tonight.

After escaping my mother, I drove downtown to Jace's Place and walked in with a big smile on my face.

"Holy shit."

Here it came.

"I'm seeing a ghost. Can anyone else see this guy? Or is it just me?" My best friend Jace stood behind his bar with a bottle of scotch in his hand, staring at me with his jaw hanging. "Somebody, anybody, tell me I'm not crazy?"

"Hey, Jace." I slid onto a barstool. "It's good to see you, too."

Someone clapped me on the back as they walked by and I turned my head to see Phil, one of the older dragons in our clan. "Welcome back, son."

"Thanks," I called. Turning to Jace, I wrapped my hands around the glass that had miraculously appeared on the bar in front of me.

"You could've kept in touch better, you asshole." Jace gave me a dark look and then poured an amber liquid into the glass.

"I know." I took a sip of the scotch, surprised he'd given me the top-shelf stuff. "In my defense, medical school was pretty intense."

Jace narrowed his eyes at me, then nodded. "Yeah, I guess it would be." He grinned and filled my glass again. "I guess I forgive you. You're here now."

"That I am." I looked around the bar, which had been Jace's dad's once upon a time. "Place looks great, Jace. You've really done a lot with it."

The bar I remembered had been a smoky, smelly hole in the wall. Jace had remodeled, filling the bar with memorabilia related to dragons, though the humans in town wouldn't be able to realize that. Accolades and awards that dragons had accumulated over the years. We tended to avoid things like participating in organized sports, but we loved coaching them. Phil had coached a college in Tennessee to a national championship in football before retiring. Rumor said they hadn't had a win since he left.

Jace had that championship trophy up on the wall, next to a photo of one of our clan who was now a high-ranking politician in Washington. Of course, most people knew he was born and raised in Bluewater, not many realized he was a dragon.

"Thanks." Jace looked around as if trying to see it with my fresh eyes. "It does look good, doesn't it?"

We chatted a bit about the accomplishments of our clan and Jace refilled my drink one more time. "You ready for tonight?" he asked.

"Ready as I'll ever be, I guess." I grinned. "We knew it was coming eventually." Not that I was upset about it.
Becoming alpha meant I'd be able to make some changes.

Do things the way they should've been all along, instead of keeping our pack stuck in the Dark Ages. I supposed my father had done what he thought was right at the time. And maybe back then it was right. All I knew is that things were different now and we had to adapt.

"I never got the details of why you left. But I always thought it was Skylar." Jace gave me a square look. "Was I wrong?"

I sighed and shook my head. "You're not wrong. Skylar's my mate. Fated, destined, all of that."

Jace's jaw dropped. "I knew it," he whispered.

"Hello, Anthony." A woman's sultry voice caused me to freeze with my drink halfway to my mouth. I looked to my right to see a gorgeous woman standing in a provocative pose, with her cleavage prominently displayed. She had long black hair and deep hazel eyes and a smirk that told me she knew it.

I'd known women like her all my life, although in this case, I'd known *her* all my life. "Hey, Tessa. How's it going?"

She practically purred as she ran her hand up the outside of my right arm. "It's good to have you back, Anthony."

I let my arm turn over, displaying my mating tattoo, which hadn't stopped throbbing since I stepped foot into the hospital the past Monday. Since I wasn't physically near Skylar, it wasn't actively burning, but a residual ache remained.

Tessa's eyes fell on it, and she knew exactly what it meant. Her breathing quickened. "Who is it?" she whispered. I read excitement coming off of her. Did she think it was her?

"I'm not sure you know her," I said. It was difficult, not rolling my eyes. There was nothing wrong with a woman who liked a good time, no more than it was wrong for a man to. But Tessa'd had her eyes on me since we were too young to think about such things. I should've known she wouldn't be able to be cool when I saw her again. She had to make it weird. She didn't just want a good time from me. If she had, I might've taken her up on it. She wanted a whole lot more.

"I know everyone in this town," Tessa said. "And I know she was someone at your sixteenth birthday party." She arched one eyebrow, challenging me.

"When I'm ready to talk about it, I will," I said firmly. "For now, just know that as attractive as you are," she preened at my words, but it didn't last long, "it isn't you."

Her face fell sour. "Well, then, you've made a mistake." Tessa flipped her silky black hair over her shoulder and turned away. "See you tonight."

When she was across the bar, with plenty of talk and music confusing the sounds she could potentially overhear, Jace leaned one arm on the deep mahogany bar. "Can it even work? With a human?"

I sighed as my heart sank deep. Practically to the floor. "I have no idea," I whispered. "My time away from Bluewater wasn't *only* about training to be a doctor, you know. I also spent a lot of time researching it."

Jace was called away to pour a couple of beers for some humans I didn't recognize. While he was gone, I thought about the things I'd learned.

"So?" Jace asked when he came back. This early in the day, the bar wasn't too busy. He had time to lean near me and talk. "What did you learn?"

"It never happens," I said. "Dead end after dead end. If it happens, it's kept so quiet I couldn't find it. I contacted clans all over the world, traveled on holidays, the whole nine yards. Not a whisper."

"Well, I know we can have sex with humans because I've done it over the years. A few times." He leered at me with his eyes full of laughter. "Quite a few times."

I shook my head at my old friend. Same old Jace. Half playboy, half jokester.

"But what about kids?" he asked. "No instances of half-shifter, half-human babies?"

I shook my head. "Nothing. If it's happened, it's been really well covered up."

Jace shrugged. "Then why did your dad send you away?"

"Old prejudices, I guess? If it's something more, he won't tell me."

"Well, still, if it's happened to you, it stands to reason you're not the first. You just haven't found anyone willing to talk yet." He filled a few more beers before returning. "So, what are the big plans now that you're home?"

I gave him a weird look. "What do you mean? What do you think my plans are? I'm going to be the alpha and a doctor. What else would I do?"

Jace returned my look. "And that tat on your arm?"

Rubbing it absently, I rolled my shoulders and gave Jace an uneasy grin. "I'm planning a few changes, once I'm in place as alpha."

Jace's grin changed his whole face. "Good. I'm glad to hear that. Time to shake things up again."

We joked around until it got later, and the sun went down. Jace had a human part-timer that worked the bar at times like this when the clan got together. Jace and I walked together to the meeting, my nerves jangling all the way.

Our ceremony was scheduled to take place on the bluffs overlooking the ocean. We were a water clan, our strength drawn from liquid, especially the ocean. We had to live near large bodies of water. It was part of the reason I'd

chosen Harvard and a hospital in Boston. It was right on the

Massachusetts Bay and kept me near the sea.

We walked to the designated shifting spot. Our clan wasn't

limited to shifting only during clan shifts, but if we were

going to all do it at the same time, we had to have a cover.

That was where our clan witch came in. Long ago, dragon

shifters and witches teamed up. We gave the witches

protection. Real witches survived the witch trials, Salem or

otherwise, and our clans tried to help as many of the

humans as we could as well.

As we crested the hill, I breathed a sigh of relief when I

caught the view of the ocean under the moonlight. "I

missed this," I whispered. There was nothing like this view,

not anywhere in the world I'd been so far.

The rest of the clan followed us, some coming from the

forest, some from the nearby fields, and a few flew in,

shifting back to their human forms and landing on the cliff. My mother and father waited at the peak of the cliff, ready to get started.

"You got this," Jace said.

I squared off my shoulders. I'd been waiting a long time for this. "I do have this." As I nodded at Jace, I noticed Sammy, our clan witch. She sat in a lawn chair at the edge of the cliff. We couldn't see it, but all of us were under a large bubble of protection. A ward.

My father put his arm around me as we faced the clan. "Tonight, we pass the alpha energy, in a time-honored tradition dating back to..." He looked at me with an amused look on his face. "The beginning of time?"

The crowd chuckled as they finished assembling in front of us, and as Dad talked about his time as the clan alpha, I looked at the people. My people. Soon, it would be up to me to protect them, make sure they thrived and succeeded;

everything. Their survival as dragons would be on my shoulders, at least until I had a child and that child took over as alpha. I secretly hoped it was a girl. We hadn't had a female alpha in a few generations, the firstborn coincidentally having been a male.

It looked like everyone had come, from the oldest—my mom's great-aunt, Gertrude, 103 years old—to the youngest, Tessa's sister's new baby boy. Tessa held him off to the side, rocking him and patting his butt as she watched my father. She'd be a great mom one day, no doubt, just not of my children.

"Anthony, are you ready?" Dad asked.

I stepped forward and smiled at everyone. "Thank you all for coming. I know I've been away for a while, and I appreciate that you've all still supported me. And to everyone who sent cards and emails and such over the years, you're so appreciated. It felt amazing to know I had the support of everyone here at home. I hope I'll prove to be as strong a leader for you as my father has." I wanted to keep it short and sweet before the actual handing over of power.

Dad took my hand and dropped to one knee. I had no idea how this would work. Dad always told me it was tradition for me not to know, that his father hadn't told him, and the clan members who had been around at that time were sworn to secrecy.

"Anthony Mason, I submit as your beta. I will follow your guidance and will in all things. I trust you to lead our clan and make decisions for us all. You are now my alpha."

The rest of the clan followed suit, starting with my mom, and ending with Great-Aunt Gertrude who slowly lowered herself with the help of her cane. "We submit as your clan," they intoned as a group. Had they planned this beforehand? How did they know what to say?

"We will follow your guidance and will in all things. We trust you to lead our clan and make decisions for us all. You are now our alpha." As the words faded, the energy in the air shifted, and a weight laid on my heart. I knew, at that moment, that it had happened. I was now their alpha. The burden settled heavily in my soul. Not a bad burden, but there all the same.

They rose and stared at me in silence. "Thank you," I whispered.

Dad got to his feet and held out his hand. "That's it."

I laughed and looked around as the hundred-odd clan members closed in on me. "That's it?"

Aunt Gertrude cackled. "Now, you must command all of us not to tell the next alpha."

"But why?" I asked.

"The pressure of the oncoming ceremony is enough," Dad explained. "Your child, when he or she becomes alpha, needs to take it seriously. But it's nothing major. There are no bangs or flashes. Responsibility comes to us all, son. And now the biggest one is yours."

"Thank you all," I repeated. "I know this is typically a hereditary thing, but it means the world that you all have accepted me. Unless something has changed, we've had no requests for transfers?" I gave my father a quizzical look.

He shook his head. "None."

That warmed me. "There will be changes," I said. "As with any new alpha. I hope to take the clan into the digital age, find ways for us to be modern and in touch with the rest of the world, but all that can wait for another day." I didn't mention other ways I wanted to progress the clan forward, either. Like mating with humans. That could definitely wait until after my very first night as alpha.

"For now, let us shift and enjoy our time together!" I yelled as my shift began.

My dragon erupted, my clothes disappearing, thanks to a spell put on me at birth by Sammy. It wasn't a completely necessary spell, but it made life easier. Sammy had invented the spell herself and I knew she'd shared it with few other witches. She was a little proprietary.

I turned and ran for the cliff, trusting our beloved Sammy to cover me as I launched myself into the air and roared. The ocean below kicked up, the frothy waves already volatile turning violent as they reacted to my innate magic and my connection to the water.

Flying high before looking back, I watched my clan follow me, launching into the air and circling below me, frolicking both with each other and the ocean. They dove into the waves, coming up with mouthfuls of fish and sea creatures, shooting arcs of water out of their mouths.

Sammy walked to the cliff, holding the only baby our clan currently had. There had been a time when we'd had several, and the mothers and fathers took turns watching the children or flying, but at the moment it was only young Wallace, watching us fly with his onyx and golden eyes that all dragon babies had.

My heart full of pride, I joined them, and we flew late into the night, wild and free.

Chapter 5 - Skylar

"Are you sure I can't get you anything else?" Cam smiled at Dr. Mason with a strange look on her face. We were near to lunchtime on a busy Monday, and the energy in the office had been odd all day.

And it had something to do with Dr. Mason. Everyone gravitated toward him.

Except me. I couldn't figure out what everyone's deal was. He was the same doctor who made everyone revamp the way they charted, even though our charts had been perfectly adequate for *years* before he came along.

"No, thank you, Cam. I appreciate the offer." He handed her the charts he'd asked her to digitize. As he turned around, I buried my nose in my tablet, hoping he wouldn't notice that I'd been paying attention.

After feeling the weight of Dr. Mason's gaze, I turned and walked into my next patient's room. I had no idea what in the world was going on with everyone today, but I wanted nothing to do with it.

My next block of time was empty, thankfully, because I was starving. I headed down to the cafe, but they were serving meatloaf. I loved meatloaf, but I hated the cafe's meatloaf. It looked like it was going to be a cafeteria day.

I hit the elevator and went down to the old part of the hospital. The hallways were quiet down here. Truth be told, I did like the cafeteria more, but it wasn't worth the risk of running into Bret.

After going through the line, I settled down at a table and put my phone on a game to play while I ate my chili. I hadn't even started throwing birds when one of my nurses plopped down beside me. "Hey, Skye," she said.

I scooted over and smiled at her. "Hey, Bernie. What's up?"

Cam slid into the seat across from us and put her tray down. "Care if we join you?"

Shaking my head, I pulled my tray close to make room. "Of course not."

They usually ate in a huge group in the cafe. Sometimes I joined them, sometimes not. In a way, I was their boss, so it was sometimes awkward for them to sit with me.

"So, you used to be close to Anthony, right?" Cam asked.

I nodded. "Yes, Dr. Mason was my friend all throughout childhood."

"What happened?" Bernie leaned forward, food forgotten.

I sighed and put down my fork. "At his sixteenth birthday party, he kissed me, then disappeared."

They both stared at me, waiting for me to continue. "Like, disappeared? A magic trick?" Bernie questioned.

Laughing, I clarified. "No, no. He pulled back, ran off, then came back a few minutes later sending everyone home. I didn't hear from him for three days, then he told me goodbye at the park, saying he was going to some prestigious school in London."

"Well, he did say at his intro meeting that he'd gone to a school in London," Cam said.

"Yes, he did." I waved my fork at her. "But he didn't have to completely ignore me, did he? No. He didn't. I wasn't in love with him or anything, but he still broke my heart. He was my best friend, literally for as long as I could remember. We made friends at the park when we were like two or something." I shrugged. "But all that didn't matter to him once he moved." Okay, so maybe I was a little bitter about it. "I'll be honest. I don't get the fascination with him."

Bernie gaped at me. "Okay." They hadn't really asked for quite that much information. She glanced at the others then back at me. "But, I mean, have you *looked* at him? He's gorgeous."

"I still see the scrawny, pimple-faced boy that helped me put straws on my bike spokes, so they'd be loud." I absolutely did not see the muscled, tall, gorgeous doctor he'd become. Nope. Not at all.

"Shush," Cam said. She looked over my shoulder with wide eyes. "It's *him*."

Ugh, he must've come through the door. I looked over my shoulder in time to not see Dr. Mason as I'd expected.

It was Bret, and his pregnant Barbie doll walked beside him. Damn it. "I thought she was staying home," I muttered. She was the perfect little trophy wife now.

"She likes to come to eat with him." Cam gave them both a disgusted look. Bret's new baby mama had been a CNA here at the hospital, working with him in podiatry. I didn't feel any envy toward them. I was glad to be away from him now, especially knowing the kind of man he truly was. But I definitely hated their guts, both of them.

Bret's gaze landed on our table, and I averted my eyes, praying he wouldn't come over.

Baby mama walked toward the line, but Bret turned his direction toward my table. "Damn it," I muttered.

He stopped at the empty chair beside Bernie and directly in front of me. "Hey, Skye. How are you?"

Bernie and Cam watched with wide eyes as I tried not to tell him to go straight to Hell. "Hello," I said in a stiff voice. I met his gaze, because looking away somehow meant I was less than.

I was one thousand percent better than Bret. I wanted to slap his stupid face and stab my fork in my ear to keep from hearing his stupid voice. He had cheated on me for most of our relationship. It took everything in me not to scream at him. "What have you been up to? I hope you've been well."

"Fine, thanks." I kept my teeth clenched together and my glare on his lying, piece of shit face.

"Mary's getting close to delivery." He stuck his hands in his pockets and rocked on his feet as if we were having some sort of relaxed, catch-up conversation.

This man had some big fucking balls. The audacity to bring up the woman he'd gotten pregnant weeks before our wedding. This son of a bitch. I opened my mouth to tell him to go to Hell when someone put their hand on my shoulder.

It was Dr. Mason. Not Anthony. To me, he would be Dr. Mason. He didn't deserve to be on a first-name basis, not even in my head. I wasn't sure how I knew, but even after all this time, I recognized his touch. It felt like electricity passed between us, but with Bret standing right there, I didn't move. I was in between two men I wanted to be a thousand miles away from.

But if I had to choose one, I definitely chose Dr. Mason. At least he'd left instead of cheating on me repeatedly.

Bret's gaze glued to Dr. Mason's hand on my shoulder. Normally, I would've pushed it away, but in this case, I was okay with Bret jumping to any conclusion he wanted to.

"Hello, I'm Dr. Anthony Mason." His hand tightened on my shoulder. "And you are?"

Bret bristled. "Dr. Bret Cooper, podiatrist."

Dr. Mason huffed through his nose, just loud enough for everyone to hear. "Podiatry, how nice. I'm a pediatric surgeon."

Bret's nostrils flared and the corners of his mouth tipped down, one of his telltale signs that he was furious. He couldn't stand the fact that someone with a more impressive specialty had their hand on my shoulder.

Cam's and Bernie's heads swayed back and forth as they watched the pissing contest, and nobody missed Dr. Mason's hand on me.

"It was nice to see you again, Skylar." Brett nodded once at Cam and Bernie. "Ladies." He walked away without saying goodbye to Dr. Mason.

Damn it. Thanks to those two men, the entire hospital would be talking about this whole exchange. I hated being the topic of gossip for anyone. I dipped my shoulder to get his hand off of it, then pushed the chair back, leaving it up to Dr. Mason to get the hell out of the way.

"Excuse me." I grabbed my tray and shoved my phone in my pocket, then made a beeline for the tray return area. The small room, off to the side of the cafeteria, was my closest escape and had a second exit into the stairwell so I could go back upstairs and eat something out of the vending machines instead of spending one more moment in this damn cafeteria.

I vowed to never come to eat lunch here again. Maybe I could get my schedule changed and start working nights. I'd have to leave primary care, but whatever. It would be worth it to not work with or run into either of the men that made me absolutely nuts.

"Who was that?"

Damn it. He'd followed me. I should've known he would.

"Hello, Dr. Mason."

"For the last time, will you please call me Anthony? It's not like we haven't known each other for three decades."

I slammed the tray down and whirled around. "Fine. *Anthony*. Who that was is none of your business. Please mind it." Damn him and his name. Calling him Dr. Mason had helped me put some distance between us. But *no*. It had to be *Anthony*. I separated out the trash from the dishes on my tray. "And why did you come over there, anyway? With your hand on my shoulder like you own me or some shit?" I flipped my hair over my shoulder and turned to meet his gaze.

"You *are* my business, Skylar."

I burst out laughing, and just like that, I'd had it. No more. "You have no right to me, or knowing me, or knowing about me." I tried to keep my voice down, but my anger spiked. "You walked out on me, disappeared after a literal lifetime of friendship and never contacted me again." I pushed past him toward the stairs. "You were my best friend," I yelled as I slammed into the door and started up the stairs as the door's bang echoed satisfactorily below me. "Do you know, I still don't have another best friend?" Anthony's footsteps echoed behind me, telling me he was still behind me. "I have friends, but I've never allowed myself to get as close to another person as I was to you." Damn my diarrhea of the mouth. Why couldn't I just answer a question and then move the hell on?

"Skylar—"

"No! I was your business once, but not anymore. I'll deal with you, because I have to work with you, but you're not a part of my personal life anymore." I whirled around and pointed in his face. He was only a couple of steps behind me on the stairwell, and he reeled back and grabbed the rail with a shocked and hurt expression on his face. "And you *never* will be again."

We'd reached the primary care floor. I slammed my way through that door and straight into my small office, shutting the door and locking it. I'd have to see him at some point throughout the day, but for now, at least I had a granola bar in my desk.

Damn Bret, and damn *Anthony*. Both of them were assholes and neither of them deserved me. I was better off alone.

Chapter 6 - Anthony

Rolling over in bed, I pulled the blankets over my head and tried to go back to sleep. It was Wednesday, my weekday off since I'd done my monthly on-call this past weekend. The clinic was open a half-day on Saturdays and Sundays and everyone took turns staffing it.

It'd just been me with Bernie and Cam there. I'd been both thankful and disappointed that I wasn't working with Skye, but none of the doctors ever worked the weekends together. Though she wasn't a full doctor, she counted as one as far as scheduling went.

She was right back in the office on Monday, though, which was the day I'd made a total ass of myself with her and her ex.

Bret. How I'd wanted to rip his face off. I'd played dumb, but the nurses had already filled me in on what happened between the two of them. When I saw him talking to her, I had to interject myself. That asshole had to know there was someone that would have her back.

But Skye hadn't appreciated it. In fact, it had made everything worse. She was my mate, and I couldn't ignore that, but that made the week packed full of tension. Her dislike for me was out in the open. I had to believe things would work out between us.

I just wasn't so confident that I had the skills to win her over. Not after all the years away with no attempt on my part to contact her.

Eventually, I fell back to sleep, waking later in the morning to the smells of breakfast.

"Anthony!" My mother's voice and the promise of coffee pulled me from the bed. "Hungry?"

I threw on some workout clothes and shuffled downstairs. "Morning."

"Afternoon, more like. You okay?" Mom looked at my face and pressed the back of her hand to my forehead. "Did you catch something at the hospital?"

I shook my head and pulled back. It was time to start looking for my own place. I loved my parents, but I'd been in town nearly three weeks now, and I was ready to make my own breakfast in my boxers or to sleep in without worrying about anyone thinking I was sick. "Mom, I'm fine. Dragons don't get sick."

She set a plate in front of me. "Well, I worry. You're around all those diseases. What if there's one that we haven't been exposed to yet?" I rolled my eyes, but she pointed at the food. "Eat up. Your father is out back, about to go for a fly. You should go with him."

That sounded nice, so I scarfed down the egg sandwich and chugged the coffee. "Okay, see you soon." I pushed the chair back as I took the last bite. "Love you, Mom."

She smiled indulgently at me. "I'll get the dishes. Go."

I took my coffee out back with me in time to see my father set his coffee cup on the picnic table on the patio. "Hey, Dad."

He turned with his eyebrows up. "About time you got up. I figured you would've outgrown the need to sleep in on your off days."

Chuckling, I gave him a shocked look. "Never. Sleeping in is the best part of my week."

He nodded toward the back yard. "Wanna go for a flight?" We owned land for miles around the house, outside of the city limits, and near the ocean. We didn't fly over the water unless Sammy was around to shield us, but we could head into the woods without fear of being seen. Sammy had long ago put permanent wards on them to discourage any humans from entering.

"Sure." I put my cup down and took off running, transforming halfway across the back yard into my dragon. All the Bluewater Clan dragons were some shade of blue or green, and we all had characteristic marks of iridescence at the tip of each of our scales, making us sparkle in the sunlight like each scale was embedded with a jewel. Even I thought we were the most beautiful of all the dragon clans.

We had several transplants to our clan, of course. If we didn't intermarry between one another, we'd be like royalty of old.

Inbred.

Tessa was descended from a mountain clan down in Tennessee. Her parents had moved to Bluewater before she was born. As a result, she was more of a deep, forest green with browns mixed in when she shifted into her dragon. She was totally a viable mate for me, but fate had decided otherwise. I really had no freaking clue what would happen if and when Skylar and I made it work and had children. Would they be dragons? It was possible it would be the end of the Bluewater Clan line. If another alpha took control, the clan would change. The energy would be different. The colors would morph over time.

We weaved in and out of the trees, dodging branches and spiking high over the tree cover before diving back down. Deer ran beneath us, content that we weren't their enemy. The legends said that when a dragon clan moved into an area, the animal population steered clear, but once it became apparent that we didn't hunt them, they began coexisting peacefully with us.

The magic in me fortified the magic in the rest of the clan. Every clan had to have an alpha, supported by his betas.

When my father stepped down, he became my beta, as did Jace. Others could be betas as well, dragons with the capacity to be alphas who chose not to try.

We turned when we reached the outer limits of our land and headed back toward the house. When we landed, we sat at the picnic table and enjoyed the afterglow-type feeling that came after a flight. It wasn't unlike the relaxed satisfaction after sex.

"How are you liking being the alpha so far?" Dad asked.

I shrugged. "There's not much to it at the moment. It's not like the old days, is it?"

Dad chuckled. "Not at all. Thanks to our alliance with the witches, many of the old duties are much more relaxed. We don't have to constantly patrol our borders or organize the clan to make sure everyone has jobs. It's really more of a figurehead position except for the fact that you're the conduit for the magic."

"I'm glad they don't depend on me like they did your grandfather or even your dad," I said. "It would've been damn near impossible to have a high-stress job like a doctor back then."

"How about your old friends? Have you caught up with everyone?"

He gave me a look out of the side of his eyes. I knew damn well what he was actually asking. "Yes, I've talked to Skylar, if that's what you're trying to say." I turned my gaze on him, the peace of the after-flight atmosphere broken.

He swallowed and then sighed. "I never liked forcing you away from her. It was a necessary thing, but I took no joy in it."

It was hard not to yell at him. "I know you think you did the right thing, Dad, but you didn't. I didn't choose Skylar. Fate did. Our ancestors, or God, or whoever it is that decides which mate is perfect for each of us. My tattoo was pretty dormant in all the years I've been gone. Since I've been home, it's blazing like the sun."

His shoulders slumped. "I've seen her around town. The guilt has been pretty bad. I should've told you years ago how sorry I was to force you to leave."

"You should've brought me home."

"I figured you would've asked if you'd wanted to come, to be truthful with you, son. Once you left, you never brought it up again."

I decided to cut him some slack. "I've always been worried about it. I hoped that I could either get some answers or time and distance or… something so that when I returned either it would go away, or we could make it work."

"And did you?"

I shook my head, hating the fact that I had to say no. "Nothing changed. No news and she's definitely still my mate."

"It drove a wedge between us. I just wanted you to know I only did it because I thought it was the best thing for you."

"I know you thought that. But you did things your way, and now it's time for me to do things my way. I need you to understand that. I don't believe fate would have chosen Skye for me if she wasn't truly meant to be mine. I'm going to do anything I can to fix things and pursue a relationship with her."

He didn't answer right away. "I still don't think it's a good idea, but you're not sixteen anymore. You're grown and can make those decisions yourself."

I was a bit more than grown, but he was right. It was my decision.

My phone beeped on the picnic table where I'd left it before we shifted. I glanced down at it to see Jace had sent a message. **You should come to the bar. I'll give you a free drink.**

That sounded great, actually. "Well, I'm going to head out. I'll talk to you later." I clapped him on the back on my way back into the house. "It'll be okay, Dad."

He stood and turned as I opened the back door. "It will be. You'll make the right decisions."

I went inside to get my keys with a smile on my face. He was going to be supportive after all.

Jace must've seen me pull in. When I got to Jace's Place, he had a cold beer on the bartop waiting on me. "For you," he said.

"I was planning to come by," I said. "Thanks for the beer."

In the early afternoon, the bar was totally dead. He walked around and hopped onto the stool beside mine. "What's up?"

"What do you know about Bret?" I couldn't keep the growl out of my voice.

His eyes flashed. "Ah, so you heard about him."

"Heard about him, saw him in action. Saw the pregnant girlfriend."

"Bret was a POS who had been cheating on Skye for a long time. They were engaged, and the wedding was just a few weeks off when he told her he'd gotten that other woman pregnant. He'd been paying for most of the wedding, and he ended up keeping all the scheduled stuff and married the woman he was cheating on her with—after getting her pregnant—in the same place, with the same caterer, and the same band."

Holy shit. Nobody had told me that. I stared at Jace with wide eyes. "You're shitting me."

"Hell, no. Bret doesn't come into the bar because I made sure he knew he wasn't welcome."

"Why would you do that?" I set the beer down and gave Jace my full attention.

"Skye and I aren't close or anything, but I have looked out for her over the years. I had a strong suspicion she was the reason your arm was shining like the sun the day you kicked us all out of your birthday party."

"I'm going to make it up to her." I didn't know how to express how grateful I was that he'd tried to keep an eye on Skye while I wasn't here. "Thank you." Simple, but effective.

Jace inclined his head, acknowledging my appreciation. "Good luck, though, man, seriously. Skye is known by most men in town for still being as tough as nails. She always was when we were kids, too. She's beaten up most of the men that we went to school with that still live in town."

I couldn't stop my smile. It seemed like not much had changed since we were kids. Well, clearly a lot changed but I was beyond glad that Skye was still *her*. I was ready to get to know her all over again.

I hung out with Jace until the bar got busier, but I nursed the same beer the whole time. I had to work the next morning and had no desire to do it hungover.

Spending the afternoon with Jace just reminded me that I hadn't spent enough time with the rest of the clan. I sent out a text before bed that night inviting anyone available to a group shift at the bluffs. I'd already made sure Sammy would be able to be there to provide us with protection.

The entire clan paid a monthly fee to Sammy just so she'd make herself available for these times. It was a pittance per family, but enough to help Sammy supplement her natural herbs and home remedies business and make it worth her while to be our clan witch.

Work the next day was much the same. Tons of tension between Skylar and me. I had no idea how to break the ice and begin bringing her around, but it would have to come down to time. What other option did I have?

My mom took the idea for the clan shift and ran with it, I found out when I got home from work. I smelled the barbeque cooking the minute I stepped out of the car in the driveway.

After walking straight through the house, I went out back to find most of the clan there, extra tables set up, and food everywhere. My stomach rumbled. "Oh, man. This looks amazing."

"Dig in," Dad called. "We didn't wait for you."

I grinned and did exactly what he suggested, filling a plate with barbequed chicken, steak, shrimp, as well as all the sides from potato salad to deviled eggs.

A strong alpha connection was good for the morale of the clan. I mingled among my people, essentially my family. When I picked up a plate of desserts, I stopped in at a different table.

"Anthony, I've been wanting to ask." My father's oldest friend, Howard, waved at me. He was also Tessa's father.

"What's up?" I grinned at the table and squeezed in.

"You've got a mate tattoo," he said, pointing his fork at my arm. "Yet you have no mate."

"I always thought it would be Tessa," his wife, Marjorie, said.

Tessa snorted from the end of the table. "I thought it would be me, too."

I sucked in a deep breath and tried to handle it in the most diplomatic way possible. "In due time, everyone will know everything but, in the meantime, you should focus on what's happening now, communion and family."

Most of the other clan members seemed satisfied by my words, but not Tessa.

"Or you could be upfront and honest with us now," she said. She stared at me with a challenge in her eyes.

"I'll tell what needs to be told when I'm ready for the information to come out. Being alpha doesn't mean you're owed any information about me." I stood and stared at Tessa until she averted her gaze. "Your behavior is one reason you're not my mate. You should be more respectful to your alpha."

Instead of deferring and looking contrite, she just looked annoyed, and I made a note to keep my eye on her.

Chapter 7 - Skylar

"Girls' night!" Kaylee's voice drifted up my stairs.

"Come in!" I yelled. "I'm just finishing up my makeup!"

The minute I got off work, I'd gone to get my hair done, and it looked great. My normal girl at the salon had done it in intricate braids and twists. I had the entire weekend off, and I was ready to let loose and blow off some steam.

Kaylee's footsteps bounding on the stairs told me she was coming up to help.

"In my bedroom," I called.

She came in looking like a million bucks, her blonde hair curled into something that looked right out of the fifties. She wore a slinky black dress that sparkled every time she moved, and higher than sin heels.

"Is that what you're wearing?" She looked so scandalized I couldn't help but recheck my outfit. I'd picked out a black skirt that hit right above the knee and a flowy blue shirt to match. "You look like a bruise."

I burst out laughing, unable to argue her logic. "I suppose you want to pick out my outfit?"

"Duh." She walked down the hall. "Put on eyeliner, I'll have something for you when you're done."

I hadn't planned on wearing eyeliner, but I knew she wouldn't stop harping me until I did as she said. She was the master of girls' night, after all.

By the time I got both sides even without looking like a total raccoon, she'd found my sexiest dress. "Well," she said with twisted lips. "You wore this one last time, and I had to make you then, too, but it'll have to do." She handed me the hanger with the slinky red dress. "We're going shopping before our next girls' night."

I tossed my shirt at her face and changed so we could head out. Bluewater had exactly one club and one bar, and they were next door to each other downtown. We parked in my dad's shop parking lot and walked across the street and down the block to the club. "I brought my key." I jangled my purse. "If we don't want to do a rideshare, we can crash in the apartment above Dad's shop." Once upon a time, he'd rented it out, but it was currently empty and fully furnished. And the perfect place to sleep off whatever we drank tonight.

"Perfect! Girls' night!" She waved her hands in the air, and I couldn't help but catch her excited mood.

As soon as we walked in, someone yelled my name. "Nurse Skylar!"

I looked around until my gaze landed on one of my patients' moms, who I'd meant to call already. Things had gotten a little crazy and I hadn't. "Hey, Bri." Kaylee and I walked over to the table where Bri was already a little glassy-eyed.

"Join us," she said in a loud voice. "It's my little sister's twenty-first birthday." She stood and looked around. "She's over there dancing with her boyfriend."

Kaylee shrugged. "Sure, thanks. Twenty-first birthdays are a lot of fun." A server came by. "We'd like Jell-O shots, and keep 'em coming, please." Kaylee slapped a twenty down on the server's tray. "That's part of your tip in advance."

The lady looked at the bill with wide eyes. "Part?"

I leaned around Kaylee and grinned at her. "Oh, yeah. Kaylee and I both waited tables in college, so we always tip well."

She winked at us. "I'll take extra good care of you."

That was the point. Kaylee leaned back and winked at me.

The server returned in no time with a tray full of plastic cups with red gelatin.

"Excellent," I cried.

Kaylee threw her hands in the air and whooped, but Bri looked apprehensive. "That's got to get expensive."

She jumped when Kaylee slapped another twenty on the table. "It's on me!"

With her job, she was free with the money and not afraid to talk about it. Kaylee entertained people online for a monthly subscription. Adult entertainment. She was damn good at her job, and as a result made quite a good income.

I'd long since stopped arguing with her about paying for everything. Every once in a while, I'd buy her something as a thank you, but she would insist on paying for most, if not all, of our girls' nights.

We giggled our way through the tray and ended up ordering another. The night was exactly what I needed. A night to unwind.

Before I knew it, I had a healthy buzz and all three of us joined Bri's sister on the dance floor.

A couple of guys tried to dance with me, but it wasn't a big deal. I smiled and pushed away from them, working my way between Bri, Kaylee, and Bri's sister, whose name I still didn't know.

After a while, I had to break for a drink. My throat was nearly sore from laughing so hard during our dance. Kaylee had been dancing like a big dork, doing the robot and the sprinkler among other dances that made me laugh.

Back at the table, one of the guys that had tried to dance with me walked up. "Hey, baby."

I chuckled and looked around for the server. She caught my eye right away. I lifted my glass, which *had* contained an appletini, and indicated I wanted another. She nodded that she understood. I'd been raised by my father and a shop full of mechanics, so I knew not to leave a drink at the table to be roofied. I'd finished my drink before heading out to dance and would finish this one before going back to join my friends.

When I turned, the man was still there. He smiled, but his gaze was glued to my chest. "Would you like to dance?"

"Thanks, but I'm here for girls' night," I said over the music. "I appreciate the offer, though." I edged to the side, putting some space between us, but he advanced when I retreated. Damn it. Guys like this were so annoying. I was entirely capable of handling myself, but it took away from my night.

"A pretty little thing like you. Why don't you smile?"

And with that, I was done being nice. "Look, you're handsome enough, but your attitude sucks. Leave me alone, please."

The sleazy smile on his face faded and it darkened. "You bitch." He didn't say it loudly. I couldn't actually hear it over the music, but it was easy to read his lips.

I opened my mouth to tell him to fuck off, but then he disappeared. Damn. How many appletinis had I had? Speaking of my drinks, the server walked up with her jaw hanging. "Here," she said.

After taking my drink, I followed her gaze to find the asshole on the floor halfway across the room with Anthony standing over him.

Dr. Mason. Dr. Mason stood over him.

"What the hell?" I walked over with the server trailing behind me. When I got closer, I saw Anthony's foot was planted firmly on the asshole's neck. Even over the noise, I heard a low rumble come from Anthony, and it vibrated through me. He leaned over and said something in the guy's ear. I couldn't hear most of it until the end when he said, "...burn you to a crisp."

I exchanged a glance with the server and realized Kaylee and Bri had walked up behind her. All three of them had matching shocked facial expressions.

"Are you okay?" Anthony put his hand on my arm and peered down at me. "Did he touch you?"

I shook my head and tried to remind myself that I was an independent woman who didn't need a man to fight my battles.

But shit, seeing him scare the balls off of that guy had been so freaking hot. It set me all atingle. "I had it handled," I said.

Anthony stepped back. "I'm going to pretend you said thank you."

"Thank you," I said. "But I had it handled."

He rolled his eyes. "I have no doubt you could have taken care of yourself. But I happened to be here, so you didn't have to."

Anthony grabbed the guy by his shirt and yanked him to his feet. "Get the fuck out of here," he said loudly enough for all of us to hear. The creep shot me a dark look before hurrying across the dance floor and out the front door.

"Can I buy you a drink?" Anthony asked.

I still had a full appletini in my hand, but after all that shit, I needed another. Throwing my head back, I downed the sweet, green drink and handed it to the server. "Okay. Buy me a drink."

Anthony grinned and led the way over to the bar, where he ordered me another drink and himself a beer.

"So, how's your night going?" he asked while we waited.

"Well, it was going great until just a minute ago." I rolled my eyes.

His face fell a little. Oh, no. He thought I meant it was going well until he came along.

"No, I meant I was having fun until that dick wouldn't leave me alone." I wasn't sure at all why I was trying to reassure him. I didn't even like him… or his chiseled jaw.

"Can we go somewhere quieter to talk?" he asked.

Oh, fine. Geez. "I guess."

He looked around. "Any suggestions?"

"There's a balcony upstairs, come on." I didn't want to see if he'd heard me, I just led the way. Kaylee winked at me from the dance floor as I passed her. I stuck my tongue out at her and crossed my eyes.

When we stepped out on to the balcony, I was glad I'd had a few drinks already. It was chilly out. "So, what do you want to talk about?" I asked.

"I just wanted to know how you've been. I understand if you feel like I don't deserve to know, but I might remind you that at one point you *were* my best friend."

I eyed him and sighed before taking a long sip of my drink. "Might I remind you that you left me and acted as if I never existed."

Anthony stared off, looking down at the view of the town. "I have a lot I want to tell you. I'd really appreciate the opportunity to explain everything, so it makes more sense."

He didn't look at me for several seconds, giving me time to consider. It intrigued me, the idea of knowing what had been the driving factor behind his decision not to reach out to me at all.

"Can I take you out to lunch one day soon?" He still didn't look at me, as if he sensed that I needed time to figure out what I wanted to do.

Not knowing what in the hell had happened had bothered me for *years*. If I was honest with myself, it never really stopped bothering me. But was it worth knowing to have to suffer through lunch with the man that caused me nearly as much hurt as Bret had?

I hadn't been *in* love with Anthony when he'd left, but the kiss we'd shared just before had definitely tugged at my heart. I had loved him, though. How could I not have? We'd been inseparable since before we were potty trained.

In the end, curiosity won. "I'll give you a chance to explain yourself."

His smile was bright enough to light up the balcony. I looked at him and pretended it didn't make my heart race. I also pretended it hadn't given me special feelings before, when I'd been so sure I wasn't in love with him. When we'd been just best friends. Practically family, even.

"Monday. Can we go to lunch together?"

I nodded and sipped more of my drink. How much of my decision to go to lunch with Anthony had been bolstered by the alcohol? Oh, well. I was in now.

"Come on," he said. "I'll walk you back to your friends. I was hanging out with Jace next door, but if you need anything, any of you, come on over. I'll stick around a while."

He didn't hold my hand, but somehow it felt like he was touching me all the way down the stairs and across to the table where Bri, her sister, and Kaylee sat with their heads together.

I didn't have to wonder what they were talking about.

"Well, goodnight," Anthony said. "See you Monday."

I nodded and smiled. When he turned and walked away, I caught the server's eye and drained my drink, then sent her a crazed look. She laughed and nodded. She knew what I needed. Anthony was just next door, and I needed more drinks to drown out the fact that I *knew* he was just next door. Like a bodyguard I hadn't asked for.

And when the fuck had I started thinking of him as Anthony?

Chapter 8 - Anthony

Skylar looked up at me with a half-smile on her face as I passed. "Morning," she said.

It was more than I'd gotten in the weeks since I'd been working with her. After leaving her at the club on Friday night, I'd done exactly as I said and went next door to Jace's. I had her scent and the sound of her body moving in that dress stuck firmly in my ears. Installing myself at a table against the wall that separated the bar from the club, I'd focused and tracked her all night. By sound, mostly. Then, when she and her friend left, I hadn't stalked them, but I'd watched from the sidewalk in front of the bar until they'd gone into her father's shop. One of her friends had walked to the apartments down the road, and Skye and her other friend had gone to one of the apartments above the shop. I knew he and Skye had lived above the shop in an enormous apartment when we were kids. I'd heard them say something about staying there for the night so I felt good about going home.

What the hell was I going to say to Skye now? I had no freaking clue. The one thing I knew was that there was no way I was ready to tell her the full truth. Not while I didn't have a clue if she was remotely interested in me. After the connection we'd had this weekend, I had hope, but hell, there was every chance that she didn't even remember that happening. I didn't want to bring it up, either, and have her give me a blank stare. I had to go slow, at a snail's pace.

As the day wore on, I was pleased to find her attitude had lightened somewhat. She either remembered the conversation we'd had or subconsciously it had affected her feelings toward me. She'd been positively chipper all day. "You're slacking," she called as she rushed past me. I had tucked myself into one of the cubbies in the hallway. They had one stool and one shelf, perfect for putting in notes and logging data.

Before I could refute her claims that I was slacking, she'd disappeared into a room. The woman was a beast when it came to seeing as many patients as possible, yet somehow, I never heard complaints that they felt rushed.

Shaking my head, I finished my notes and headed into my next appointment with my stomach growling. Breakfast hadn't stuck with me today.

An hour later, I was tucked back in the cubby, logging the notes for the four appointments I'd managed to squeeze in before the office closed for lunch. They always took an hour and a half, which was a nice change from what I'd had at my last hospital, where it was grab lunch on the go. This way gave us time to play catchup and eat, and also room to squeeze in an extra few appointments during flu season or other times of emergency.

"Are you still there?" Skye asked as she closed an exam room behind her down the hall. "That's the same spot you were in the last time I saw you."

I shut off my voice recorder and backed it up two seconds so the transcriber wouldn't pick up Skye's teasing tone. "Yes, but I did manage to take a few appointments in between. When do you chart?" I looked at her as she walked past, but she just waved at me.

"During the appointments," she said. "I don't leave a room without putting most of the notes in." Her voice echoed in the quiet office. All of the nurses and staff were down eating lunch. "Are you coming?"

Grinning, I threw down my recorder and hurried after my mate. She did remember. "Let's slip out of the hospital," I suggested as we reached the elevator. "If nothing else, it'll help keep us from dealing with stares or whispers."

Skye nodded and reached up to twist her hair up and put a clip in it that she'd pulled from who knew where. She didn't carry a purse. One of those girly things, I guessed. "Plus, if my ex shows up, that would cause more drama." She sucked in a deep breath. "I haven't been following the advice of my favorite teacher in medical school, anyway."

"What advice was that?" I asked.

"Always leave for meals," she said. "Whenever possible, get out of the hospital."

"Makes sense. It would help with the fatigue just walking out in the sunshine halfway through the day." The elevator ride was comfortable, which was an enormous improvement from even the last week. My inner dragon, the wild part of me, was more at ease the more time we spent with Skye without any strife between us. A mate was like a tether that kept the magical side of me steadier than I had been in years, even though I had a good hold on it before. Now, the shaky world had settled itself, and the base of it was between Skylar and me. My heart thumped in anticipation of what it would finally feel like to claim her.

"You've got to figure out how to do all these appointments," she said in a teasing tone.

"What do you mean?" I asked. "I got them done just fine."

She nodded and I followed her off of the elevator. "You did, but you had fewer appointments than I did, and if I'm not mistaken, you're not finished with your notes, are you?"

I narrowed my eyes at her as we stepped out the front doors of the hospital. She was still full of spice. She'd always challenged me when we were kids, too, keeping me on my toes and pushing me to be ever better no matter what we did.

"Let's not talk shop," I said with one eyebrow raised. "Besides, you could give me a few more weeks to acclimate. I'm used to being in an operating room far more than a sick room." And it hadn't been the easiest thing to get used to. I longed for those days that I'd signed up to pick up a few shifts over in the main part of the hospital. Most of those shifts were just appys and gallbladders, but still. "Where would you like to eat?" I asked before she could jump back in and give me shit. But I did it with a smile on my face, so she knew I wasn't truly avoiding the subject. We continued down the sidewalk toward the small shopping center across the road from the hospital that included several restaurants and a couple of food trucks.

Nurses and other staff from the entire hospital loved to come over here to eat. I noticed people noticing us and realized our attempt at avoiding stares had failed.

Still, walking around with Skye made me feel like a kid again. Light and carefree.

"Let's grab a coney," she suggested.

I wrinkled my nose and gave her a crazy look. "Are you nuts? It'll take me an hour to get back on my feet and go to my next patient with a loaded hot dog in my stomach. How about the deli?"

Eating heavy during a work shift made me queasy. Always had.

Skye burst out laughing. "As much as you eat, you don't want a heavy meal for lunch?"

I shrugged and looked at her out of the sides of my eyes. "I still like to eat a lot, but putting a big greasy meal in my gut, then doing a surgery just always feels gross."

She turned toward the deli. "Well, that's fine. I can do a sub."

I ordered a chopped salad, and Skye got an enormous meatball sub with chips and a huge drink.

When she plopped her tray down, I couldn't help staring at her. "I remember you barely eating… ever. I always felt like a pig around you."

She grunted and took a big bite of her sub. After chewing thoughtfully, she shrugged. "I guess that's one of the few things good that came from my relationship with Bret."

At least there was something. "What do you mean, did he teach you how to eat?" I laughed and mixed in a little dressing with my salad.

"No, but when we first started dating, before we'd even had a meal together, he asked me what was one thing I disliked about the opposite sex in regard to dating and stuff. I said I hated how guys seemed to so easily drop girls and disappear." She arched one eyebrow, and I winced.

"Okay, how does that relate to food?" I asked.

"He said he hated when girls pretend they don't eat when he knew darn well they went home and chowed down. Apparently, that was something his older sister always did, and he saw the latter half of it, where she would come home and eat everything but the refrigerator, starving after her date."

I nodded thoughtfully. "I never thought about that. I've had dates and hookups and stuff, but I've never lived with a woman."

Her jaw dropped. "Never? How is that possible at your age?"

I looked down at my chest. "I figured I'd be bleeding from that direct hit." I mimicked clutching at my heart. "That one hurt."

Skye burst out laughing and the sound of her mirth lifted my spirits even higher. "Well, it's true. You didn't have a real relationship in all this time?"

Stuffing my mouth full bought me a few minutes to think of a reason that wasn't centered around her being my mate. "Nope." I went with simple. "I spent all my time focusing on my work and school before that."

"Well, that's understandable, I guess." We got quiet, both of us eating and thinking about how we'd spent the last two decades. I was, at least, and assumed she was until she blurted out her next question. "Why did you leave, really?"

Thank goodness I'd just taken a bite. I set down my fork and chewed thoroughly, then made a show of wiping my mouth and getting a drink. "It was very complicated." I didn't want to lie, but neither could I tell her the full truth. I gave her all the honesty I could. "My parents thought I was losing focus on the important things in life and felt sending me away to clear my head was best for me and my future."

She didn't like that one bit and narrowed her eyes. "Was it me that was causing you to lose focus?" she bluntly asked.

Well, I'd decided to go with honesty. "Yes."

The hurt flashed across her face, and I quickly backpedaled. "But not in the way you likely think. There was a lot of pressure on me, and my family felt like I wouldn't be able to live up to my *full potential* because there was one thing I wanted more than anything." I didn't say the rest of the explanation, leaving her to suss out the meaning of my words.

She stayed quiet for a long time before she nodded. "I can understand why your parents wanted you to focus. Look at what you've become. Would you be the doctor you are today if you'd stuck around? We shared one kiss, and to be honest, it rocked my world. If you'd stayed, would we both have finished high school with honors?" She chuckled. "Well, I assume you did. I did."

I nodded. "Yeah. Valedictorian."

"Hey! Me too!" She laughed, but it faded, and she still looked sad. "It really hurt me when you ghosted. I didn't understand why you just cut off all communication. I still don't understand, but I have a better idea."

I tried to think of a reason. Nothing that came to mind really worked. "I don't have a reason," I whispered. "Leaving hurt me, too. Significantly." She met my eyes again as I spoke. "Every time I thought of contacting you, it made me want to cry." That was the truth without saying the rest. That I'd wanted to cry because I knew she was my true and destined mate and I couldn't have her.

She went quiet again, and I focused on my food. I wanted to stare at her and watch how the light coming in the window danced over her features, but that would've been a little awkward. "I've decided not to hate you anymore," she announced. "It's in the past and your parents did what they thought was best for their teenage son. I can't hold that against them." She cocked her head and smiled. "Or you. I'm ready to move on and for us to really be friends."

As my heart warmed, my tattoo started to burn sharply. Even with the pain, my dragon felt even more settled. It was like a wave washing over me. Could the whole clan feel it?

"I'm really glad to hear you say that," I whispered. "I would like to move forward as well, and maybe make up for lost time." A few seconds later, I got a text. "One sec, sorry." The tone told me it was my mother and she never texted me during work hours.

Did something happen?

"Sorry," I muttered as I typed out a quick reply. **No, why?** "My mom's ears must've been burning."

Skye waved me off as she took another big bite. I glanced at her puffed out cheeks and grinned at my phone as

Mom's reply came in. **Several members of the clan felt something odd. Like a wave of happiness.**

Sorry, that wave came from me. Tell everyone I'll try to mask my emotions more. I'd been warned about this. I'd have to do a better job of keeping my waves of happiness to myself. But this even further assured me that my parents and ancestors had been wrong. A dragon could have a human as a mate, and I was even more certain that Skye was truly mine.

After Skye proclaimed that she was no longer angry at me, the rest of the day went even better. She stopped in one of my exams and showed me how she charted during her exams.

I hated it and vowed never to do it. How did she split her attention so well, so that the patient didn't feel ignored? If I tried that, all my patients would complain about my bedside manner. I continued catching up on my notes and ended my day a good half hour after my new friend.

And mate.

As soon as I finished, I left the nearly empty office and went straight home. "Dad, Mom," I said by way of greeting as I walked in. They were at the kitchen table, waiting for me to have dinner.

"Sit," Mom said. "I just laid it all out."

I helped myself to an enormous plate of food. Mom knew I didn't eat much at the hospital. She'd prepared a feast. "Thanks," I said gratefully. "I'm starved. But there's news." As I scooped more food onto my plate, I blurted out what had given me such a wave of happiness. "I'm surer than ever that Skye is my mate. The tattoo has burned all day, and every time I'm near her, it's brighter and stronger."

Mom and Dad exchanged a look. "But that means exposing humans to shifters," Dad said uncomfortably. "At the very least, if you're sure, you have got to tell the clan. Nobody can be blindsided by something like this." He sucked in a deep breath and set his silverware down. This had upset him, as I'd been afraid it would. "I'm worried it'll give the younger shifters ideas about mating with humans. The bloodlines can't be sullied by that much human blood. If we start procreating with humans, if that's even possible, our bloodlines could start to dwindle."

I couldn't have given my parents an explanation, but as my dad rambled about mixed-breed babies, I knew it wouldn't be a problem. I had no science to back it up. I hadn't been able to find anything in all my searches to indicate I was correct. But I *knew* I'd be able to give Skye babies. And those babies would be shifters.

"Call a meeting," I said. "For tonight. All who can come."

My parents froze, my mom with a bite halfway to her mouth. "Now?" she asked.

I continued eating, as if at my ease. "Now. I want this out there. They need to hear the news and start getting used to it."

Grabbing my plate, I refilled it quickly and left the room. I knew my mom would start the phone chain and get as many people as possible at the meeting, but I didn't want to talk to them about it anymore.

***

The weather was perfect for flying as a clan. My family and friends milled about while I waited for as many people as possible to arrive. We'd been lucky that Sammy had been able to come to provide us with some cover or flying after I talked to everyone wouldn't have been a possibility. Finally, when it seemed like waiting any longer would be a stall, I held up my hands. The clan, keyed into my mood, quieted and gathered around. I stood on a stump. "Thank you all for coming with such short notice. It means a lot. I had confirmation today, that you all likely felt, that I've found my true mate, and I wanted to tell you as soon as possible."

Titters of emotion ran around the circle of people, but I continued before anyone could say anything. "When I was sixteen, I kissed a human and my mating tattoo appeared. I knew then that she was my mate," the circle erupted in protests and gasps, but I carried on after raising my voice, "but in an abundance of caution, my parents had me go away. I've done the research. I've studied. And I can find nothing to say there's anything bad that will happen by me taking a human mate. It's not like I have much of a choice anyway. The magic has chosen her for me. My dragon is absolutely bent on mating her." Finally, I stopped and let them have their reaction.

"I don't see it'll be a problem," Jace said loudly as everyone else looked horrified. The crowd stepped back and looked at my friend. I would've kissed him if I could've reached him.

"I agree." To my shock, my mother stepped forward. "I think the decision we made all those years ago was the wrong one. Who are we to question what the magic has decided? Are we that arrogant? Do we believe we know better than fate? Than destiny?"

My father's face grew darker and darker. I knew he didn't agree, but as long as he didn't give us a bunch of crap about it, it wouldn't matter.

"And," my mother continued, "I trust Anthony and his judgment."

Tessa snarled at me, her sour expression catching my gaze. She'd had a thing for me for ages, and I knew it hadn't lessened. But what was I supposed to do, ignore a fated mate for a somewhat hateful clan member? No.

"You're a fool," she hissed. "Forget that human. Be true to your clan."

Several people agreed with her, but they were the fools. Not me. "A fated mate is different from a chosen mate; I can't force my heart to be somewhere it doesn't belong. I'm going to pursue Skye, and I won't let anyone get in my way." I didn't leave any room for arguments, layering my special alpha magic into my voice. "Now, let's fly!"

Chapter 9 - Skylar

My sandpaper eyes made it really hard to remember why I agreed to pick up a morning shift on the main hospital pediatric floor. I had to be there at six, as opposed to the normal eight thirty-ish.

Those extra two hours were murder. Absolute murder. And once again, I was out of coffee. I spent way too long searching for the other bag of light roast I could've sworn I bought before giving up and driving to the hospital with my eyes propped open. I didn't have time to stop at my favorite coffee shop. The hospital cafe had to do. It was okay, though, their coffee wasn't terrible.

I regretted my decision not to stop at the cafe about ten seconds after I ordered my large coffee. As I stood beside the counter, trying to convince my eyelids that being open was a better state than they were currently in, I heard the worst sound in the world.

"Hey, Skye. How was your weekend?"

My ex's voice grated at my nerves, making me want to grit my teeth and slam his head into the counter.

Maybe I was still a little bitter. Just a tad. "What do you care?" I shot over my shoulder.

I was cranky, but I hadn't had any coffee. Nobody should have to deal with Bret sans caffeine. Or ever.

"Come on, Skye. Don't be that way. I'll always care for you."

My eyes finally opened as his words struck me. Freaking hilarious. "Go care about your new wife."

The barista gave us both a wild-eyed look and handed me a big cup of coffee. "Thanks," I whispered. I had cream and sugar in my office, but I wasn't headed to my normal job, so I had to stop at the station and get some, giving Bret another opportunity to say something.

"Is this how it's going to be? Will you ever move on?"

I sighed and tried not to turn around and pour my scalding hot coffee in his face. "Bret," I said without turning around. "I have moved on. I have even forgiven you. I simply dislike you and don't want to see you or speak to you. Is that too much to ask?"

Apparently, it was, because as I walked away from the cafe, Bret followed. "Skye, what happened wasn't planned. I didn't intend to fall in love with Mary. Or for her to get pregnant, definitely. I felt obligated to marry her after getting her pregnant."

His whiny voice was just simply more than I could take. I whirled at the elevators after pressing the button. Hopefully, the lift came quickly. "Bret, you're a lying, cheating piece of shit. I hope your wife realizes what total scum you are and leaves you. Soon."

To punctuate my words, the elevator dinged behind me. I turned and stepped on. "Don't follow me," I hissed as I jabbed at the close doors button.

Although it felt good to say those things, my encounter with Bret soured my already sleepy mood. As soon as the coffee cooled enough, I started sipping it. If I was going to be sour from my Bret encounter, at least I could be awake.

I got to the floor and was met by the department's usual NP. "Hey." I looked around. "Was this not my day?"

She gave me a blank look. "Yeah, but my schedule opened up. They were supposed to call you."

So here I was, and nobody needed me. The hospital paid me by the hour, but I was salary over at the clinic. "Okay." I gave her a tight smile. "I'll just head over to the clinic." I might as well get some time in over there now that I was up early and awake, kind of. I had some paperwork I needed to do, anyway.

I gripped my coffee and tried not to walk like I had a stick shoved up my ass. I was beyond aggravated, but it wasn't her fault. There was no telling whose fault it was, and I wasn't one to want to hunt down the poor clerk or nurse who had dropped the ball.

Even though I didn't want to come down hard on one person didn't mean I was in a better mood. When I got to the office, it turned out we'd had two nurses call out, so I ended up putting on my RN hat for the day. Not that I minded, but it didn't make me any less cranky to find out they needed me all day.

"Enough of this." A couple of hours into my day, Anthony cornered me in an empty exam room as I finished changing out the drape over the exam table.

I set the drape down and faced him in surprise. "What?"

"Everyone is complaining about you today. You do realize nobody asked you to work today, right? We would've muddled through, even down two nurses."

I glared at him. "I thought I'd help out."

He nodded and checked his smartwatch. "Fine. Come on." Reaching out, he snatched my hand and pulled me from the room. I didn't ask where we were going as he dragged me through the offices and out into the waiting room. I had been pretty crabby, so he obviously thought I needed some lunch. It was the right time for it, anyway. My stomach was rumbling like crazy. "Maybe a nice sandwich will put me in a better mood," I muttered.

The elevator went up, to my surprise. I looked at Anthony with my eyebrows raised. There wasn't anywhere to eat above us.

Anthony held up his hand and when the elevator doors opened on the top floor, he took my hand again and we walked around the corner to the stairs. He banged the door open. I considered questioning him, but it was pretty obvious we were going to the roof. I just wasn't sure why yet.

He banged that door open, too, but as soon as we stepped out into the bright, warm, sunlight, he stuck out his foot, then bent over, balancing on one leg. "On TV shows, when they come onto roofs, they always get locked out," he explained after he picked up a large piece of cinder block and put it in the doorframe, so the door stayed cracked open. "It seemed better safe than sorry."

I let out the first laugh I'd had all day. "I think I've seen that show."

Anthony took my hand again and pulled me forward. "Come on."

"Can I ask what we're doing?" I arched an eyebrow and looked around at our small town. The hospital serviced several counties nearby, otherwise, there wouldn't be nearly enough people in Bluewater to justify such a large medical center. I spied my dad's body shop through the trees, the spring growth still thin enough to see most of Main Street. In a few weeks, the bright green leaves and budding flowers would obscure the details.

"Scream." Anthony spread his hand out, indicating the vast open space in front of us.

I peered over the side of the roof to the parking lot six stories below. "Excuse me?"

"You are in the worst mood I've seen since I came home. And for once, you're not yelling at just me. It's everyone. So, I thought you might need a good scream." He indicated the view again. "What better place to do it?"

He had a point, but it felt so silly I looked at him askance. "Scream."

"Seriously." Anthony laughed and turned to face the open air. He opened his mouth and bellowed, sticking his chest out and holding his head back. I jumped a little at the sudden loudness, but then couldn't stop the giggling. He faced me again after a good, long yell. "Laugh all you want, but I feel better. Just be careful not to yell so loud or hard that it makes your vocal cords sore."

"Yes, doctor," I said through my giggles. It was too hard to do with Anthony staring at me, so I paced and looked out at the town.

And remembered Bret's words from this morning. "Bret is trash, you know?" I spoke to Anthony, but I didn't look at him. "Total scum. He made me feel loved and cherished and like everything would work out beautifully. His betrayal was a complete blindside. Which," I started shaking my hands and picked up steam, "I should've seen

coming. All the warning signs were there. But no, I had to

be naive and now I have to see him *every fucking day*. He

cheated because I wouldn't give him a baby."

My inner turmoil and rage bubbled up inside me. I whirled

and faced Anthony. "And I wouldn't give him a baby

because I *can't have them*!" I screamed the last words,

totally ignoring his warnings about my vocal cords. They

rubbed together as my words turned into a raw scream, and

the pain of never being able to bear a child erupted from

my mouth.

When I finished, the silence beat at my ears like a drum. I

stared at Anthony, challenging him to say something about

the secret I'd revealed.

Instead of speaking, he walked forward and reached up. I

stopped myself from flinching and was surprised when he

wiped my cheeks tenderly. I hadn't even realized I was

crying. "What do you mean you can't have children?" He wiped his hands on his pants, though for a split second I thought he was going to lick the tears off his finger.

Weird.

I shrugged and sniffled, wishing I had a tissue. As if he'd read my mind, Anthony pulled a handkerchief out of his pants pocket. "It's wrinkled but clean." He held it out.

I took it gratefully and wiped my nose. "I have PCOS."

He took the handkerchief from me and folded it over before dabbing under my eyes at the tears that continued to fall. "PCOS doesn't mean no kids. It's not the end-all, be-all."

Folding the handkerchief again, he continued dabbing without coming too close or touching me in any other way. His actions spoke of boundaries and caring.

I appreciated it more than I could say, his respect for my bodily autonomy. Lifting my gaze, I stared into his eyes as he continued to speak. "Maybe the universe knew that Bret wasn't meant to be the father of your children."

His suggestion warmed my heart but also tickled that tiny sliver of hope I kept stamped down and under control. I knew there was always a chance of children, but it hadn't happened in years with Bret, even though we never used any sort of birth control.

He thought I was doing it on purpose. I never could bring myself to tell him the truth. Maybe there was a reason for that as well.

Looking deep into Anthony's eyes as he lowered his hand was nearly too much for me. He parted his lips slightly, and when his tongue darted out to moisten them, I shuffled forward a half-step. I leaned forward ever so slightly just as Anthony stepped away.

Son of a bitch. I'd been about to go for it. Talk about an about-face. I'd gone from hating his guts to lusting after his lip moistening.

His gaze was still on me, and for a split second, his eyes looked like embers, like coals banked in a fire. He blinked and it disappeared, but I would've sworn he'd reflected flames. I looked around the roof, but nothing remotely resembling a fire was up here. Damn. Must've been a trick of the light.

Something felt so off to me, but I'd just broken down on the rooftop and screamed my deepest secret to the world. My emotions weren't to be trusted at the moment.

Anthony held out his hand again. "Let's go eat something while we've got a break, yeah?"

I nodded and took his hand, and the spark I'd seen in his eyes flashed between us as soon as we touched. My brain was so focused on the fact that I almost kissed Anthony and the disappointment that it hadn't actually happened that I almost missed how hot his hand was.

"Anthony, you're burning up," I exclaimed.

He pulled his hand out of mine and looked at me in surprise. "Am I?" Before he reached for the cinder block to open the door, he leaned over. "Feel me."

I nearly snorted. I wanted to feel him all right. So much for hating him and barely forgiving him. I pressed the back of my hand against his forehead, but he was cool to the touch. Confused, I snatched up his hand again.

There was no excess heat. "I guess I'm a little woozy from all the yelling," I said weakly. "Let's go eat."

He grabbed the block and then held the door open for me. As I walked through, I reminded myself he had betrayed me. I wasn't in the market for being his bestie again like nothing had ever happened those years back.

No matter how hot he was. Literally or figuratively.

Chapter 10 - Anthony

"It's time for me to get a place," I announced at breakfast on Saturday morning. "Well, move into my place."

I'd been working on it all week; I just hadn't had the nerve to tell my parents. There was an old stone house on the outskirts of clan land that I'd purchased years ago. I knew I'd need to move home eventually, and when the property had come available, bordering my parents' large acreage, I'd jumped on it. Over the years, I'd rented the house out to clan members. When my tattoo had flared up again when I moved home, I started the process of helping the current tenant find another place to live.

And now they'd vacated, the cleaner had come through, and it was ready for me to move in.

I was more than ready. My mother was about to drive me insane asking about Skye. And every time she did, Dad stiffened and cleared his throat, changing the subject.

"Skylar and I shared a moment," I said after my mother asked me about Skye for the hundredth time this morning.

Dad sighed, again, so I kept going to get all the news out at once. "And I've arranged to move into my house. It's ready for me."

They knew what it meant. My bond with Skye was growing. At this point, there was no ignoring it whatsoever. The more time I spent with her, the more my feelings grew and intensified.

And this son of a bitch *burned*.

What came next was unavoidable, not that I wanted to avoid it, anyway. It was time to deepen the bond and pray that she reciprocated my feelings. If she were a dragon, we'd likely already have been mated. I would've given her my bite and that would've been that. But she was human and sinking his fangs into her neck just wasn't going to fly. There was no precedence for telling a human about us, not that I'd found so far, anyway. As far as I'd seen, it hadn't happened.

"Well, I've got most of my things packed, and arranged for the rest to be brought from storage. I'll head over after breakfast. Let's arrange a clan fly for anyone available this afternoon?"

Dad nodded with his attention on his breakfast. "Did you contact the witch?"

His gruff voice irritated me. He'd been in a foul mood since I came home, nearly. Definitely since I announced my intentions for Skylar. I ignored his tone and answered his question. "Sammy is free this afternoon. That's what made me want to see if anyone can meet. Though, I'd like to try the bluffs behind my new house. It's a great spot, if I recall correctly."

Mom cut her eyes at Dad. "Okay, darling. I'll make the calls. Say four?"

After swallowing my last bite of French toast, I gulped down my juice and headed upstairs. I didn't have all that much stuff here at my parents' house, a few books and clothes. I got it together quickly. Mom was in the foyer when I brought down the last suitcase. "You know," she said. "You lived away from home for so many years. Now that you're leaving again, I find I'm upset about it. I don't want to see you go."

I set my last suitcase down and put my arms around my mother. "At least this time I'm just down the driveway. Not several states or countries away."

She laughed. "You're right. And you still hate doing laundry, I'm sure. You'll be back."

After giving her a squeeze, I jaunted out to my car, in a great mood.

By the time the first of the clan members began pulling up in their various vehicles, I had my suitcases unpacked and had explored the house. It was the first I'd found time to get out there since coming home.

I spent most of my afternoon going around and ordering random items I knew I didn't have in storage, like a plunger, mop, and dishwasher tablets.

It would all be delivered in two days' time. In the meantime, I'd make do and hope I didn't need the plunger.

A handful of clan members turned up along with my mom and dad. It was a nice number to try out flying from my new place. "Welcome," I called when Sammy walked up. She was so petite that I was lucky I didn't overlook her so far away. She nodded her head, and her short black hair didn't move. She'd had it cut close to her head, shorter than

I'd seen it last time. She smiled and waved as she opened up her lawn chair. I made a mental note to order something special for her when I got back inside. The woman was a saint for looking out for us. When she waved again, I knew we were protected, so I addressed the crowd. "I don't have any news, so we can get started!"

After everyone murmured their assent, I grinned and shifted before launching myself off the cliff. It was an even more secluded spot to fly. Our normal location had a small beach at the bottom of the cliffs. On hot summer days, we liked to fly down to the beach and enjoy the privacy of a spot otherwise only reachable by boat. These bluffs had only rocks and more ocean beating against them at the bottom.

Soaring through the salty air, I marveled at the feeling of bonding with a clan again. I'd missed this in Boston. Flying had been a few and far between experience, reserved for when the local clan alpha remembered to shoot me a text and invite me to join them. I tried shifting in my home a few times, just to take the edge off, but it was less than satisfactory without taking to the air.

Flying with a strange clan had been a bit like eating a peanut butter sandwich when I craved steak. It filled me up and did the trick, but this, being with my clan and family, this was steak. Steak and shrimp.

If I could add my mate to the flight, that would be the whole meal. I'd be sated. I lost myself in the journey, banking and diving, using the water, and playing with my clanmates. I even tried diving into the ocean, which was not as fun as I thought it would be, and I remembered only after trying it that the last time I'd done it, I'd said never again. Hopefully, the next time I got a hair up my ass to try it, I'd remember.

When the sun dipped below the horizon, reflecting off the water, I glided back in and landed in the large open swath in front of my new-old house. As I shifted back, everyone else landed around me. I turned to Sammy, who had stood and folded her lawn chair. She waited for the last person to shift back before giving me another wave and walking down the lane.

I never asked how she got here, but I'd also never seen her car. The woman was a mystery in a tiny package.

It took nearly an hour to tell everyone goodbye. They all stopped to shake my hand, and after giving my mother a big hug goodbye, it was just me and Jace. "Well," he said. "I better go relieve the little shit at the bar. He's probably burned the place down by now."

I chuckled and shook his hand, then watched as he climbed in his car and drove away.

The sun had long since set, and the moon was rising higher and higher in the sky. I walked slowly toward the house, happy to see the outside lights worked, and came on as soon as I was in range. One thing to tick off my to-do list: Checking the motion sensor lights.

As soon as I went in, I headed for the shower. Taking my time under the hot water, I thought about the flight and wondered if it would ever be possible for Skye to fly with me. Would my bite turn her? As I soaped up and rinsed off, the possibilities of what might happen once I bit her ran through my mind for the hundredth time.

It all came down to uncertainty. There was no telling what my bite would do to a human. None whatsoever.

As I toweled at my hair and stood dripping in the bathroom, my cell phone chirped in the next room. When I dried, I wrapped the towel around my waist and tied it off to go see who had texted me.

It was Jace. **Skye is here at the bar with her friend**
Kaylee.

I picked up the phone and replied. **So?**

His reply came first with several emojis indicating booze
and laughter. **Kaylee is wild. They're likely to get tanked.**
Thought you'd want to come to play bodyguard.

Seconds later, he followed up with, **You enjoy playing**
bodyguard.

Well, he wasn't wrong about that. I didn't need telling
twice. Without hesitation, I threw the towel and got
dressed, thanking my mother for drilling neatness into me
as a kid. If I hadn't unpacked earlier, I'd be searching now
for something to wear and wasting precious time.

Clad in jeans and a tee, I grabbed my leather jacket and
hopped in the car.

Even though my place was a good drive outside town, I got there in no time. As soon as I walked in, I knew exactly where Skye was, at a table near the center of the room. But I purposely didn't look over there. Instead, I headed for the bar with every cell in my body sure that Skye's gaze was on my back.

"Thanks," I muttered as I sidled up to the bar.

Jace chuckled and nodded toward their table. "I was right to call you; she might really be needing a bodyguard soon."

I chanced a glance in their direction, and sure enough, Skye's gaze was glued to me. I gave her a quick head nod, but even as fast as I looked away, I didn't miss the line of colorful shots in front of each of them.

"They come in now and then. Sometimes they go next door." Jace set a longneck in front of me. "I always make sure both of them get home safe when they come here."

I picked up the beer and tipped it his way. "I owe you for that."

He waved me off. "You'd do the same."

As a matter of fact, he was right. I would've done that for any female that I came across who was too intoxicated, and most men, for that matter. But I didn't say that. I still appreciated what he'd done all these years while I was away.

Every time I thought about my time spent in Boston and not here, I regretted them. I could've come home years ago. Should've.

As the women drank, laughed, and cut loose, I kept my distance. But it became easier to watch her as time went by because she noticed less and less. Eventually, I was able to watch Skye and her friend openly. I wasn't sure she was able to even see the bar, much less me sitting at it.

It gave me too much time to notice the smile I'd missed seeing and the laugh I'd missed hearing. My chest ached with how much I'd missed her when I was gone and how much of our lives we missed out on. I nursed the same beer as Jace came around to check on me.

And when men began to approach, I stayed on high alert as the girls sent one guy after another on their way. I couldn't help but be amazed and proud of how well Skye handled her liquor. She went from being out of her mind silly with her friend to sober and polite to the men, thanking them for their offers but declining. At least all the men had been respectful. I didn't think she'd be very happy about me interfering in her girls' night, but if push came to shove, I would've.

As she sent the third guy off, I remembered she was raised by her dad and the guys at the shop. More than likely, she could drink anybody here under the table. Any human, anyway.

The moment she surpassed tipsy, I jumped up and swooped in when she wobbled. Skye looked up at me with her big eyes and to my delight, grinned. She wasn't upset. "Need a hand?" I asked.

"Well, that would be nice. I need to use the restroom." She patted my arm and whirled, barely staying upright. I didn't want to help her any more than she might need. She'd come here to have some fun alone, not to have me take care of her. I followed behind as close as I dared. "You've gotten even more handsome over the years," she said over her shoulder. "Really grew into your nose." Since she was sort of looking behind at me, she wasn't watching where she was going.

I fought a laugh and put my hands on her shoulders, carefully steering her toward the bathroom. "You always told me I would." I'd had more than one person tease me about my nose as a kid. I'd been all angles. Elbows, knees, Adam's apple, and nose. Every time someone had upset me, Skye had been the one to calm me down.

"Here you go." I pushed the door open for her and looked away, then stood outside the bathroom and waited. Thankfully, she made it back out without needing any assistance. When she clutched my arm, her hand was soaking wet and I smelled flowery soap. Good. She'd managed to wash up, though she'd skipped drying off. I chuckled and walked with her back to her table, where Kaylee was talking to some guy who looked like he belonged in a rock band, or maybe a biker gang. Whatever it was, he had a lot of piercings and tattoos.

"Hello," I said as my eyebrows pinched together. The pincushion glared at me.

"Anthony," Kaylee squealed. "This is my boyfriend, Luke. He's taking me home."

"You've been drinking?" I asked the man, and stood as tall as I could as I let my alpha magic flow off of me. The man wouldn't know what it was, but he'd feel intimidated.

"I don't drink." He snarled one lip at me, but I was sure he was telling the truth.

I nodded and watched Kaylee and Skye say goodbye.

"Are you taking my girl home?" Kaylee asked me.

"I'd be glad to," I replied.

She poked me in the chest. "Take care of her." Skye was busy saying goodnight to the server and stuffing a bunch of cash in her apron, so she didn't notice.

"I will. You have my word."

Kaylee nodded and winked and walked toward the sober Luke. I watched them walk out, then put my hand on Skye's elbow. "Come on, I'll drive you home."

She waved to Jace on the way out, and he gave me an exaggerated wink from behind the bar. I rolled my eyes and flipped him off over my shoulder. "What's your address?" I asked as I opened my car door and helped Skye sit down without bumping her head. I felt like a cop helping a prisoner into the car. Chuckling, I circled to the driver's seat.

Skye rattled off the address when I got in. "Why don't you know where I live?"

I turned over the engine and looked at her out of the sides of my eyes, mainly focusing on the road. "Honestly?" Not that she'd remember this. I plugged the number into my GPS. "I intentionally didn't find out. If I knew where you lived, I might've been tempted to drive by and see you all the time."

She grinned at me and leaned over and slumped against the window. Her eyes slowly closed, and in seconds, she was asleep.

Good grief. She was cute and funny now, but I hoped she didn't drink like this all the time. At our age, especially, it could lead to real problems. When we pulled into the driveway of the house, I stopped and stared at it. We'd been riding down the road parallel to the beach on our bikes and we'd pulled over in front of this little cottage. She'd told me then, all those years ago, that she wanted to buy this house and fix it up when we were grown.

And she had. She let out an indelicate snore at that moment, and all I could do was laugh, half in happiness at how cute she was and half with sadness. I'd promised her

I'd help her fix up the house. We were going to move into it as soon as we'd graduated high school.

Something else I'd missed out on. Another sharp pain hit my chest, a pang of regret.

I got Skye out of the car and tried not to get turned on as she leaned heavily on me. We walked toward the door. "Keys?" I asked.

She shook herself more awake and dug her keyring out of her purse. I hadn't even thought to make sure she still had that. Whoops.

"Lock up when you're inside, okay?" I watched her fumble with the key but refrained from taking it and doing it for her.

She finally got the door open, and the smell of citrus drifted out. The house was dark, too dark even for me to see, but the smell stirred up old feelings of familiarity. It smelled like her bedroom she had at her father's house.

No way I was going inside. If I went in, I didn't think I'd be able to talk my dragon back out. But Skye didn't walk in. "What is it?" I asked softly.

"I wanted you to kiss me on the roof and I don't know how to feel about it." She cocked her head and looked up at me, her face bathed in moonlight. "I think I'm supposed to still hate you a little even though I said I wouldn't." Her face twisted into what she surely meant to be a mean-mug, but in her intoxicated state, it was just cute. "I've hardened my heart to men but there you are, messing with my head."

"I promise, it isn't my intent to mess with your head. I just decided what I genuinely want is you in my life in whatever capacity I can have you." I stepped closer and touched her chin with my finger. "You're my person, remember?" We'd always told each other that as kids after she'd watched some TV show where they were each other's *person*.

I'd always wanted her to be my person, in all ways, but I'd let my family ruin it.

She smiled, a nostalgic expression, before grabbing my collar and yanking me close. I allowed her control. Just because I was alpha didn't mean I had to be the one running things all the time.

But then she melted against me and seemed to submit. My alpha dragon totally took over and pulled her up in my arms. Her feet left the ground, and she moaned into my mouth as my tongue darted forward and claimed her mouth. It was heated, passionate, and more than I could take.

I put a stop to it before she could feel just what her kisses were doing to me, pressed against her stomach.

"Lock up," I said, and my voice sounded more dragon than man. It was more growl. On top of that, my tattoo burned hotter than it ever had before, and higher up my arm. It was significant enough pain to make me yank up my sleeve and glance down at it in front of Skylar, though she couldn't see it.

It had grown and was nearly from wrist to elbow now. That had to be a good sign.

"Good night," Skylar said, on her own feet again. She stood on tiptoes and pressed her lips to my jaw as I stood stiffly and tried to talk myself out of picking her up and carrying her to her bed.

I waited for the sounds of the locks engaging before stalking to my car.

I needed another shower.

And a damn good jerk-off.

Chapter 11 – Skylar

"Ugh." I rolled over in bed and tried to banish my memories from my mind.

No matter what I did, my head pounded and the taste and feel of Anthony's mouth wouldn't leave me.

Why didn't I drink wine last night? I never remembered what happened when I was wine drunk.

Moaning, I rolled over again and sipped water from the cup on my bedside table. I'd gotten up sometime in the night and grabbed it.

At least it was Sunday. If I'd had to get up and go to work, I would've been screwed.

Oh, speaking of that, I knew exactly what to do to fix my hangover. Stumbling out of bed, I shuffled into the living room and grabbed my medical kit. Twenty minutes and several attempts later, I was back in bed with an IV bag resting on a pillow above my head. I dozed while the IV rehydrated me.

It was cheating, but hell. What was the point of being a medical professional if I couldn't take advantage of some of the perks?

When I woke again, I felt much better and the bag was nearly empty. I carefully took the IV out, disposed of everything, and slapped a waterproof bandage on my wrist.

After a shower, I felt even closer to normal, though I still couldn't stop the constant replay of the kiss.

If I stayed home, all I'd do is focus on how turned on I'd been. The only reason I hadn't spent all night with my vibrator was the large amount of liquor I'd had in my system. I'd passed out as soon as I hit my mattress.

Before I rethought it and settled back in bed with said vibrator, I grabbed my keys and headed out the door.

Only to remember my car was still parked in town. I'd intended to walk to Dad's shop last night and sleep there, but when Anthony offered to take me home, all thoughts had gone out of my head.

Everything except inviting him in.

I changed up my game plan and opened the rideshare app. Ten minutes later, I was in the back seat of a woman's car who kept giving me strange looks in the rearview mirror. "Aren't you Skye?" she asked.

I nodded and smiled at her as nicely as I could with the last remnants of the hangover headache pounding through my head. She would've seen my name when she accepted the call for a ride.

"You don't have a car?" the woman asked.

She was rather hateful. I opened my app and checked her name. Tessa Bridges. It did sound familiar. "I do," I answered carefully, "but I left it in town last night."

The scenery rushed by as we headed toward Main. It seemed like she was driving really fast. This was one woman that wouldn't be getting a very good review. She was quiet for a while, so I checked email and my social media accounts.

After a few minutes, I noticed Tessa's head move. She glanced at the GPS. "You left it at a bar? Do you drink a lot?"

"Not really," I said absently as I went back to the email about a new drug from the hospital CEO I'd been reading. "We've had more girls' nights than usual here lately, but it's a coincidence."

She sniffed. "I see."

"What's it to you, anyway?" I asked. Who was this woman to make me feel judged about how often I drank? I'd been out a few times recently, but normally it was once a month, *maybe.*

"I'm friends with Anthony," she said. "I just want what's best for him."

Of course. Just my luck to call a rideshare and get the one person that wants to defend Anthony.

"Anthony isn't a factor in my life," I said. "So, whether or not I drink doesn't affect him whatsoever."

Thank goodness, I spotted the bar and my car in the late morning sunshine. "Here it is," I said. "I paid on the app."

She pulled her sedan beside mine, and I jumped out before she could say anything else. I darted around my car and got in with my phone in my hand.

Before I even turned the engine on, I texted Anthony. **Who is Tessa and why is she quizzing me about how often I drink?**

Once I hit send, I pulled out of the bar's parking lot and went across the street and up the block to Dad's shop. When I parked and checked my phone, I had a reply. **What in the hell are you talking about?**

I told him what had happened and grabbed my purse. His reply pinged as I got out of the car. **I'm so sorry. I'll handle it.**

I'd have to ask him to give me the full story behind it later. But for now, Cooter had already spotted me. "Look what the cat dragged in!" he crowed.

Dad walked out from behind a big truck and grinned at me. "Come to visit your old man?"

I nodded and smiled. "Thought I'd make us Sunday dinner." And I'd known damn well he and Cooter would be working in the garage, probably with a game on in the background. Sure enough, they had the TV mounted on the far wall on with some race cars going around and around a track. Ah, wrong sport. It was racing season.

"Come on inside," he said. "We can finish this truck tomorrow."

Dad and Cooter led the way into the house he'd built behind the shop. I headed toward the kitchen, but Cooter waved me off. "Go watch the race with your dad," he said. "I already put a roast in."

Laughing, I shook my head and plopped down. Dad had already turned the race on. "How was girls' night?" he asked. "I expected you to stay at the apartment over the shop."

"I got a safe ride home," I said evasively.

"I heard that a certain someone took you home last night." He turned his attention away from the race and fixed a glare on me. "Are you falling into his trap again? He left you heartbroken before."

"Dad, remember we were just kids."

His face darkened. "I don't care. You were hurt and I won't ever forget it."

"Okay, I won't either. But I have forgiven him. And you should too."

He pushed back in his recliner and grunted. But he didn't disagree. After a few minutes of watching the cars go round and round on the pavement, he glanced at me again. "I can't stand to see your heart broken again. Not after Anthony and then what Bret did to you." He inflected Bret's name with a drop of venom.

He disliked Anthony, but he *hated* Bret. And I didn't mind that he did. At least Cooter was busy in the kitchen. If he heard Bret's name brought up, he would've started cussing.

"I promise I'm being careful, Dad. Nothing has happened." I couldn't stop the kiss from flashing through my mind again. And my damn cheeks heated up.

"Oh, ho," Dad said triumphantly. "Then why are your cheeks red, tell me that?"

I clapped my hands over them. "They're not!"

He chuckled, knowing he'd won. I was just grateful he wasn't nagging or building up enough steam to start yelling. Then I would've had to yell back, and it would've been a whole thing.

"Baby girl, all I want is for you to be happy. That's all I've ever wanted. If that means Anthony, then I'll suck it up."

He watched the race for a few laps, but something told me that wasn't all he wanted to say.

I was right. When a commercial came on, he turned in his chair and fixed his dark brown eyes on me. "I'm telling you now. If he hurts you again, I'll castrate him."

Chuckling, I scooted to the edge of the couch and leaned over until I reached his cheek for a kiss. "Thank you, Daddy. *If* I decide to pursue anything with Anthony, and then *if* he hurts me, you'll have my full permission."

"And me!" Cooter yelled from the kitchen.

So, he had been listening after all. "And you, Uncle Coot."

He continued grumbling, but Dad just shrugged. I couldn't hear what Cooter was saying. In a few minutes, Dad startled me when he spoke up again. "Damn right!"

Whatever Cooter had just said about Anthony, Dad agreed. It was surely something that would make me roll my eyes, so I didn't ask. I sat back and enjoyed the rest of the day with Dad and his cantankerous best friend.

***

I sat in my car in the hospital garage until the last possible second. I'd stopped for coffee at my favorite shop, so all I had to do was rush in and go straight to the first exam room.

Facing Anthony after trying to suck his face off was the last thing on my to-do list I wanted to actually accomplish. If I could go the whole day without seeing him, that would've been fine with me.

Anthony was the first man I'd kissed since Bret. I absolutely hated that I was drunk when it happened. Damn it!

I watched the clock and munched on a muffin I'd picked up at the coffee shop. Knowing I'd have to acknowledge and talk to Anthony had my stomach rolling.

Damn it. I was acting like a teenager again and it was strange that I responded this way to a man, to Anthony of all people, after feeling so much nothing for so long. As soon as I finished the muffin, the clock turned over, giving me five minutes to get through the garage, across the parking lot, through the lobby, up the elevator, and into the peds office.

I made it in four. Damn it. I counted down the last minute outside the elevator, finally heading in when the clock rolled over. Immediately, I got to work and didn't see him as I went through my chart for the day. As I was getting ready to check the rooms for prep, I sensed his presence before I even saw him. It was like a magnet being pulled through my back, and it was too strong to ignore. Our eyes connected down the hallway and my worry disappeared. He walked towards me, and the closer he got, the stronger the pull felt. The sensation was overwhelming, but I didn't let on that I was affected at all. Schooling my face into a pleasant smile, I gave Anthony a little finger wave.

"How was the rest of your weekend?" He looked down at a tablet and tapped at it.

"I hung out with my dad," I said, trying to effect an air of nonchalance.

He nodded and put his hand on an exam room door but stopped and smiled at me. "How's the hangover?"

I couldn't stop the blush any more than I'd been able to when my dad asked me about Anthony. "I don't get hangovers."

He just smiled and it was almost like I could tell what he was thinking.

"Stop thinking about it." His mind was on the kiss and I damn well knew it.

"I can't think about anything else." He smiled from ear to ear, a true Cheshire Cat grin.

"You can just forget about it," I declared as I pulled up my first patient.

"No way in hell," he said loudly. "That was the highlight of my move back."

I glared at him. "I was drunk. I'd rather not our first kiss since we were sixteen be while I'd been drinking."

He held up his hands with the tablet in one. "Okay. Fine. You win if you'll have dinner with me on Friday."

"Deal," I said with every intention of bailing on him.

"I see what you're thinking," he said. "If you cancel on me, I'll make your life here at work hell." He had his jaw set and I believed him. Then, he licked his damn lips again.

"Fine!" I said in a near yelp. "I'll go." I slid around him and darted into the first exam room before he did anything else like lick his lips or ravish me in the middle of the hall. Or something.

Chapter 12 - Anthony

I hoped I'd been subtle enough. All week I'd been trying to flirt with Skye but keep it under the radar, so it didn't trigger her to push me away or otherwise overwhelm her. I'd also hoped to keep her excitement level about our date up high without wrecking it by going overboard.

But seriously. I was like a puppy dog with a new bone. All I wanted to do was wag my tail.

I'd made reservations at the Catcher in the Rye, the nicest, and one of only two proper restaurants in Bluewater. They had a decadent cheesecake dessert menu, and it had been the restaurant I'd wanted to take Skye to when we had our first real date.

But then I'd left and totally thrown both of our lives off course.

Finally, *finally,* it was time to close up shop. My last patient left, and I had three hours before time to pick up Skye. I stopped by the nurses' station and turned in my tablet. "Ladies, have a wonderful weekend." I winked at Skye, then grinned from ear to ear when she lit up as red as Christmas lights.

The nurses returned my goodbye and I headed out. I wanted to ask Skye to walk down with me, but that was bordering on encroaching into too much. I forced myself to straighten my spine and keep walking. I'd see her in a few short hours.

Besides, I needed a shower, and a haircut. Whistling, I headed out to the garage, then straight to the barbershop. I hadn't been back here since I was a kid, but it didn't matter, because it was a new owner.

I showed him the haircut I liked and twenty minutes later, I jaunted out a few ounces lighter and quite a bit itchier. Next door to the barbershop was a florist.

Perfect.

I headed in and got a bouquet of flowers I remembered Skye liking. When I checked out and headed out the door, I nearly ran right into Tessa. "Oh, hey, Tessa." I kept my voice hard. I'd already had to call and yell at her for interfering and talking to Skye.

She stared at the sunflower and rose combo in my hand. "It's sweet that you're buying flowers for your mom."

I sucked in a deep breath and tried not to get irritated. "They're not for my mother."

Her sweet smile turned to disgust. "Are you seriously going to mate with a human?" Her voice was far too loud for the middle of the street in town.

"You need to lower your volume," I said in a low, growling voice.

She didn't lower her voice at all. "Do you understand the doors you're opening up? There are whispers from the other guys about mating with *human* women. What about them?"

I grabbed her arm and pulled her as gently as I could—when I actually wanted to throttle her—toward my car. Behind it, in some relative privacy, I let go and stepped back enough that I could breathe again. "What in the hell are you talking about?"

"Don't forget it's the males who feel the pull of their fated mates. Females don't feel it until the bond grows. Human females are probably less likely to recognize it or feel it at all!"

This was wasting time I could've been getting ready for my date. "Can you get to the point?"

She sighed in exasperation. "If the males are choosing human mates then the female dragons are left with no chance of having a fated bond." Her eyes went a little wild. "Do you expect us to just settle for human males that we can't even tell about our true selves? We can't tell a human if he wasn't our true fated mate. We'd be living lies or going without companionship. How can you do this to us?" Tears coursed down her cheeks.

"I'm not against you mating with a human male," I exclaimed, then remembered and lowered my voice. "If you love and trust him, I don't see why you can't petition to tell him."

Her face reddened, and she started breathing so fast I worried she was going to lose control and shift right there in the street. "You know how human women dream of their wedding day? They plan everything from the time they're very young."

I nodded. I'd seen the movies like everyone else. "Well, female dragons dream of the day they get their tattoos. We plan for it. We imagine a million scenarios. We look at boys our age and wonder if it'll be them. But we know it won't happen until we're invested in a relationship. We worry we'll invest in the wrong one and pray our mate will tell us ahead of time. We pray we'll know early, though most women don't."

The burn of her words cut deep. I understood her anger. It wasn't the first time I'd heard a female dragon describe yearning for her tattoo. "Tessa, truly I am sorry. I didn't choose this fate, but I won't regret it. Fate chose this path for me, but I already love Skye."

She scoffed and stepped back, disgusted with me. "You're not the alpha I thought you'd be." She stormed off, her heels clicking all the way down Main. I couldn't shake the feeling of being bereft. The melancholy didn't leave me as I got ready for my date. For the first time all week, my entire focus was not on my upcoming date. Instead, I couldn't stop thinking about Tessa's words. Was she right? Was it wrong of me to tell the world that I was going to mate a human? What if all the men started choosing human females? Based on how I'd felt since I got my mating mark, there was no way that I could've ignored the call of a true mate if she were in the vicinity. The only way I'd been able to do it was by moving away.

If a dragon male developed the mate tattoo for a dragon female, there would be no possible way he could've ignored it in favor of a human.

Still though, if more dragon males began mating human females, where would that leave the dragon females? Males and females of the dragon species were born at a very even rate. There wasn't a statistically significant number of either sex born more than the other.

That would leave dragon females with the need to find human mates.

That wasn't to say all the dragon males in the clan would start running off to meet humans. I would've bet that a large majority of them would only date dragon females. To the extent that they would take a year and visit other clans in the hopes of meeting their fated dragon female mate. It's what I would have done had I not imprinted on Skye.

My inner thoughts stayed with me until I pulled onto the long road by the beach. When I pulled into Skye's driveway, my mind went back to its pre-Tessa state. The anticipation of the date.

I rang the doorbell and waited with bated breath. Skye answered and as soon as I spotted her, all my breath left me. Any coherent thought I had fled my mind and all I could think about was her beauty and grace.

I didn't know one kind of makeup from another, but Skye obviously did, because she'd done something to make her green eyes pop almost as if the irises were some sort of 3-D. "Are you wearing contacts?"

She burst out laughing. "Why would you ask that?"

"Because your eyes are more beautiful than I've ever seen them." I cocked my head "No, that's a lie. The day of our first kiss, at my birthday party, that was the most beautiful I ever saw your eyes."

She blushed, and the color only served to intensify the effect of her makeup. "Well, this is a bit much to do every day."

"You look beautiful every day." I thrust the flowers forward awkwardly. "These are for you." Smooth. Who else would they be for?

I debated calling the whole thing off and just taking her back inside her house and sinking my teeth into her neck right then. Of course, an erection tried to pop, which would have been a disaster if she noticed. "Ready to go?" I had to get out of here before I gave into my base instincts.

"Sure! You know you don't look so bad yourself." She reached inside and put the flowers on the table. "I noticed they put water picks on them so they will keep until we get home and then I can arrange them in my vase."

"I remember how much you used to like arranging flowers." That was part of the reason I bought her flowers and not chocolates.

"I still do," she said. "But my current arrangement is getting droopy, so this is perfect timing."

I led the way to my car and opened her door for her.

"Thank you, sir." She batted her eyelashes at me, and once again I had to force myself not to scare her to death by biting her in the neck.

The ride to the restaurant was thick with tension and I tried to ignore the scent of arousal in the air, but he couldn't fight a smug smile from creeping up on my face from knowing she was as aroused as I was.

I remained a gentleman for the entire night, despite how difficult it was to do so. During our date, I learned more about her time in school and what she'd been up to.

"I'm sure nothing compares to a long surgery, but I've never been so tired in my life as before the big test in med school," Skye said.

I burst out laughing. "No, you're right. I've done some really damn long surgeries. But nothing compares to the all-night cram sessions in college."

I sobered up after that and stared at her across the table as she finished her dessert. "I hate that I missed that time in your life. We should have been doing those cram sessions together. I am so sorry that I left, and I'm so sorry that I left without another word."

She put her fork down and gave me a long, serious look. "I really regret the things that we missed out on. But it's time to move forward. We can't get back the time we lost, but I'm in a place now after renewing my friendship with you over the past few weeks that I'm ready to move forward and not miss any more time."

My feelings for her settled deep in my bones as she kept talking.

"I'm so glad you're back in my life," she whispered.

The entire night went like that, a back-and-forth between us, reminiscing, talking about our lives apart, and commenting on bringing our lives back together. Before I knew it, it was time to head back to her house. I walked her to her door and looked down into her still-popping green eyes. "I'm not even going to pretend like I don't want to kiss you."

She grinned, her lipstick long since worn off, and I was grateful that she never thought to reapply it. As she went up on her tiptoes, I leaned forward and pursed my lips just enough so that they pressed against Skye's with a very gentle pressure, as if my lips were caressing hers. She melted into me, her body molding against mine. There was no way she didn't feel the evidence of my arousal. A growl erupted in my chest and the need to sink into her was almost unbearable.

"Would you like to come inside?" She unlocked the door and stepped inside, then flipped on her overhead light.

I stared over her shoulder at the interior of her home, stricken. If I went in there, I did not think I could stop myself from doing things she was not ready for. God knew *I* was ready for them. "I want to. More than I can say," I said in a low, gravelly voice. "But if I come in there now, I'm going to move things faster than we are ready for." Lie, I was so ready. "Can I just call you tomorrow?"

Her face fell, and she looked hurt.

"No!" I exclaimed. "It's not that I don't want to. Please believe that. But I don't want to rush anything, not with you. Right now, you are the most important thing in my life." I reached forward and grabbed her hand and lifted it to my lips. After giving her the slightest of kisses, I let go of her hand and stepped back. "I'll call you tomorrow."

I backed away down her walk, leaving her chest heaving and heart pounding, then whirled and forced my feet one in front of the other to my car. Then, I headed straight home and left my keys in the driver's seat. As soon as I exited the vehicle, I erupted into my dragon form and launched off the side of the cliff. I should've made sure I was covered, but the darkness would have to do it. It was cloudy, with no moonlight, and that was just going to have to be good enough.

Chapter 13 - Skylar

Well, shit. I stewed on it all night and when I still didn't know what to do the next morning, I texted Kaylee and Bri on a group text. **Do either of you have plans tonight? Wanna come over for some girl talk?**

I was so not in the mood for alcohol, but I needed advice in the worst way. I just hoped Kaylee didn't have a date and Bri could get a babysitter at short notice. Actually… I pulled my phone out. **Bri, you can bring Hayden if you don't have a sitter.**

Turned out, Bri could get a sitter and she was happy to switch her plans from organizing her pantry to girl talk with me. And Kaylee responded like an hour before Bri was due to arrive saying she'd just woken up and wouldn't mind a bit of the hair of the dog that bit her.

They arrived at eight, each with a bag in tow. "Where's the corkscrew?" Bri asked. "We're spending the night, right?" She blew her black curly hair out of her face and grinned as she held up the bags in her arms. Glass bottles clanked inside them. "'Cause I need a night where I'm in a safe place and can drink and do whatever without somebody creeping on me."

"That's fine," I said. I'd spent the day cleaning up and making the place hospitable. "I've got a guest room and one of you can either sleep with the other, or with me, or on the couch."

Kaylee winked and walked toward the kitchen. "Come on, Bri, I know where the wine glasses are."

"None for me," I called.

Kaylee stopped dead and turned to stare at me. "What do you mean none for you? Are you pregnant?"

I gave her a flat look. "You know damn well I'm not pregnant, and it's kinda shitty of you to joke."

Her face fell. "You're right, I'm sorry. It slipped out without me thinking about it." She disappeared in the kitchen, but then returned seconds later and threw her arms around me. "I love you, SkyePie." She'd called me that since I'd eaten an entire apple pie at a dinner with her one night. I didn't mind, I was pretty proud of that accomplishment.

I smacked a kiss on her cheek and stepped back. "It's okay. No, not pregnant, I've just been drinking too much lately, and I don't want another hangover like I had the other night. It's cool, though, you two go ahead."

When we got settled in with the chips and dip that Bri brought and the wine that Kaylee brought, we got down to the nitty-gritty. I explained about our kisses, my attraction to Anthony, then I had to go back and give Bri the full rundown about what had happened between us when we were teenagers. And what hadn't happened.

When I finished the whole long, sordid story, they agreed on one course of action.

"You've got to go for it," Bri said.

Kaylee nodded. "What is life if you don't take risks? Sure, it might end up badly, but then you'll get over it. If you don't try, you never succeed." She took a long sip of wine. "Enjoy yourself, but don't have any expectations."

"But it's not smart to ignore your feelings," Bri added. "Not with your history. Don't ignore what your gut tells you *and* you need to know what Anthony is feeling. With the kisses, I don't think he wants to be *just friends* with you."

"I need to talk to him. I need to know where his head is at." I sipped my water and contemplated when it would be possible to see him. If I waited, we'd be back at work Monday. Tomorrow felt like so far away.

"Go!" Kaylee exclaimed. "We've had several glasses of wine, but you haven't."

I blinked repeatedly at my friend, then looked down at myself. "I'm a mess." My hair was in a messy bun, and I'd just thrown on some leggings and an old t-shirt.

"You're fine," Bri said. "Go talk to him. If you don't come home, we'll eat your food and drink this wine we brought and go to bed."

Why couldn't I? I didn't mind leaving them here to enjoy the evening together. It wasn't like I was bailing on them and leaving them alone. They had each other. "Okay," I said excitedly. "I'm going to do it."

I jumped up and changed clothes quickly. I wasn't about to go in leggings. Kaylee and Bri followed me to the bedroom and grinned at me like tipsy fools while I slapped on a layer of mascara and put my hair into a less messy bun.

I stopped short as I slathered on some clear lip balm. "Wait," I said. "I don't know where he lives."

"Oh, he lives near my parents, near the rest of the cult," Kaylee said.

I shot her a sharp look. "Don't call them that."

"You've got to admit," Bri said. "There's something weird about them and the way they seem to stick together like they do."

I knew the town gossip. I'd heard it all of my life, but I ignored it because I knew Anthony and even though his parents weren't the most welcoming of me, they never stopped Anthony from being my friend. Not until he moved away, anyway.

But more than that, I knew Anthony, even if it'd been a long time since we were close. "Whatever. I've got to talk to him."

Kaylee leaned over. "Well, *go.*"

Bri nodded. "Yeah, stop wasting time!"

I ran for my car and headed straight for the road Kaylee's parents lived on. I'd been to their house a couple of times, and I'd been to Anthony's parents' place. If he lived near them both, I had an idea of what road he lived on.

And until I pulled into his driveway and saw his car sitting there, I was fine. It wasn't until I knew I was in the right place that I began to panic.

Shit. Maybe I should've called first. Just showing up here wasn't the best idea. What if I was wrong about him? What if he had a woman over and I was interrupting something? Damn it.

His front door opened, and he stepped out onto the front porch with a confused look on his face. "Hey," he called. "What are you doing here?"

My worries faded because he looked so happy to see me. There was no denying the pleasure on his face. I stepped out of the car and stood uncertainly. We stared at each other for a long moment before Anthony stepped aside and gestured for me to come in. But I didn't move at first. I stood beside my car and looked up at the porch at him. He was just close enough that I didn't have to yell. "I have to ask you something before I come inside."

He didn't speak but watched me as I tried to gather my words. "You were my best friend and the first boy I ever kissed. The first boy I ever loved. My heart broke when you left." My heart thumped hard with the memory of the pain. "I'm terrified you'll just break it again. So, I need to know what you want from me. Why are you back?" I sucked in a deep breath. "If you're here to break me all over again, because I don't think I can come back from piecing my heart together again." His face crumpled as I spoke. It hurt him to think about how much he'd hurt me. I knew he said he'd been hurt by leaving also, but it had been his choice, not mine. If it'd been up to me, we would've stayed together. "I was sixteen, but there was something then that told me, something that made me so sure that you belonged to me. I can't explain it now, but—"

Anthony cut me off by rushing down the stairs and gathering me into his arms. He pressed his lips to mine and moaned against me, then proceeded to kiss me senseless. His tongue warred with mine and my body responded like this was the thing I'd been craving all my life and only just now realized it.

Anthony was mine.

"I have no intention in this world of leaving you ever again. You felt that because you know just like I do that you are mine. You were mine then and you're mine now. And you'll be mine until the end of our days. I'm not letting you go. I'm not breaking your heart. I want you for always."

My relief pulsed through me, a physical thing, because I *felt* the truth in his words. So, when he kissed me, I kissed him back with matching fire and passion. When he picked me up and carried me into his house, I didn't protest. In fact, I encouraged him with a moan.

The bedroom door banged open as we barreled through. The taste of him was addictive, and I didn't think it was my romantic side fooling me. I was in danger of becoming dependent on this man.

I got my hands under the edge of his shirt, breaking away from his lips long enough to pull it off. Anthony's skin was deliciously smooth under my fingertips. I shivered with need at the sight of him. He was warm, nearly feverish, but I brushed it off to the desire built up inside of him.

How did he make time with his busy schedule to keep up that incredible physique?

Then his fingers deftly navigated the buttons of my blouse and it, too, fell to the floor. He trailed kisses across my cheek, my jaw, down my throat. I threaded my fingers into his inky hair, whispering his name. Heat washed over me when his lips blazed a path across the tops of my breasts, and then suddenly they were free. He tossed my bra on top of the growing pile of discarded clothing.

"So incredible," he murmured against my skin. "Stunning."

His tongue flicked out across my nipple and my breath hitched in my throat. I wanted this. His sweet words, his hungry touches, his soft lips. I wanted him far too much for patience. Pushing him back to sit on the edge of the bed, I sealed my lips to his again while I unbuckled his belt, whipping it out of the loops in one smooth motion. Anthony groaned and grabbed my thighs, pulling me onto his lap.

His hard dick pushed against me through his pants, and I ground on him. Our breaths mingled, tongues dancing wildly. My head felt light in a way that had nothing to do with how much or how little I'd had to drink. One of his hands slid under my skirt, massaging my thigh, as he ran the fingertips of his other hand up and down my spine. My fingers fumbled with the button on his pants. I was getting entirely too worked up.

Applying the slightest pressure, I pushed against his chest until he lay back. His blue eyes shone in the moonlight coming through the window. He was absolutely the most gorgeous man I'd ever set my gaze on. Licking my lips, I slowed myself down enough to get his pants undone. Both of his hands rubbed my thighs, and it was proving difficult to concentrate.

Climbing off of his lap, I tugged his pants off, dropping them unceremoniously to the pile. I slid my hands up his thighs and my tongue over his straining cock. The salty-sweet taste of his skin made me hungry for more, but he didn't give me a chance to take it. With a growl, he grabbed me and pulled me up to him. My skirt rode up again as I straddled him.

Anthony brushed his fingers across my cheek. "Are you sure, Skye?"

I'd never been so sure about anything in my life, and I wanted to say as much, but the words wouldn't come.

Instead, I nodded and leaned over, kissing him hard. He took that answer as intended and rolled us so that he was on top. I could feel him pressing against me and reached down to pull my skirt off, but he stilled my hands.

"Wait," Anthony said, smiling. "I kind of like the skirt."

Oh, the skirt was totally staying on.

He moved away again and latched onto one of my breasts. I gasped and arched into him, heat pooling low in my belly. Again, his fingers slid up my skirt, this time grabbing my underwear and slowly pulling them off.

I wanted him to move faster. My need for him was a beast that only he could soothe.

His fingers teased my entrance, then slid in, his thumb brushing over my clit with each pump. Grabbing his hair, I pulled him back to my lips. His fingers felt so good, but it wasn't what I *wanted*.

"Mmm, you're so wet."

"For you," I replied huskily. "I need you in me."

He chuckled, then disappeared from my grasp. I blinked the lust-filled haze from my eyes in time to see him dive beneath my skirt. As soon as his tongue swiped across my sex, my mind blanked. The only thought left was the ecstasy of his touch that left my entire body tingling.

My breaths came out in quick pants as he alternated between fast and achingly slow strokes. Just as I approached the edge, he pulled back, pushing my skirt up.

Yes, please! "I'm on the pill," I gasped out, not wanting to give him even a minute longer to wait.

Anthony positioned himself, running his tip through my slickness. I closed my eyes and moaned with impatience that quickly turned to rapture as he slid in and filled every last crack in my soul. My eyes opened again to find him watching me, something like wonder combined with lust on his face. I wrapped my legs around him and pulled him closer, urging him to move.

And move he did.

It became heated quickly as he pounded into me relentlessly. I clenched tight around him, taking in every second of that delicious friction. He slowed down, and for one disappointing moment, I thought he'd finished already.

Then he sat back, grabbing my hips, and sliding us to the edge of the bed. He pulled my legs up to his shoulder, kissing my calves before he resumed his ruthless pace. With my thighs squeezed tighter together in the new position, I felt him even more. I felt every thrust hit deep, sending jolts of pure pleasure coursing through my body.

"A-Anthony!"

I cried out as an orgasm built up. My chest tightened with anticipation. The room was filled with the sound of our bodies colliding over and over, our panting breaths, our desperate desire for each other.

He grunted as I squeezed my core as tight as I could, his thrusts becoming brutal. I didn't care how sore I might be the next day. It was everything I'd been craving from him. We could do slow and sweet later, if there was a later.

Right then, it was everything I'd hoped for.

His breaths became unintelligible words that my ears didn't have the capacity to comprehend just then. My world exploded into bright lights, my chest expanding with the first deep breath I'd taken all night. Rightness settled over us, and it was an odd feeling that I couldn't ever recall feeling with another partner before.

Anthony's paced finally slowed, his thrusts turning into more reactionary jerks as my insides clenched and unclenched around him, coming down from my own orgasm. Drowsiness swept over me, and I couldn't tell if it was from the alcohol or the physical exertion.

As Anthony's warmth curled into my back, I let it take me into the darkness.

Chapter 14 - Anthony

When the sun first began to appear far on the horizon, it bathed the world in a beautiful orange, red, and pink glow. I sat on the back porch and watched it peek through the trees as I listened to the soft sound of Skye snoring upstairs.

My chuckle was loud to my own ears in the predawn quiet. I couldn't help myself though, I really had not expected her to snore as much as she did. I made a mental note to convince her to have her tonsils and adenoids checked out.

The need to bite her was so overwhelming that at the moment I was not sure I would make it through our night without doing so. I managed to persevere, a good thing since she was still clueless about my true nature.

Besides the obvious, one cool thing that came from our night together was that my tattoo was not burning at all this morning. I was going to have to tell her soon about who and what I was, or the next time this happened I wouldn't be able to stop myself.

Surprise! I'm a dragon and you're my mate. And the proof is in this bite, yeah... not the way I wanted to break the news. It would be more likely to break her mind.

I trusted that she wouldn't leave me. I trusted that she wouldn't break our rediscovered bond. But that didn't stop a small bit of fear from creeping in.

When the sounds of her sleep growing more restless began to creep in, I got up and made a fresh pot of coffee and then started breakfast. We had definitely burned enough calories to deserve a decadent breakfast, so I started crepes and bacon.

After such a wonderful night, it was time to tell her everything. She'd never be more receiving of my unbelievable news than after a night like that. I hoped. My nerves were all over the place, but I knew in my bones that it was time.

That didn't stop me from changing my mind a hundred times before she even set foot on the floor.

When I heard the bed creak, indicating she'd sat up, I started the finishing touches for our food. By the time she shuffled in, looking flushed from head to toe as she made her way into the kitchen, I had everything hot on the table.

"I promise that I don't make a habit of showing up at someone else's place unannounced."

Laughing, I set a cup of coffee in front of her. "I believe you. But you can show up at my home at any time." That wasn't technically true. If she showed up during a flight before I told her the truth, well, that would be bad. I sat beside her and dished out our plates.

"What are your plans for the day?" As I made breakfast, I'd made sure my schedule was free and clear so that I could spend the day with her. Jace and my mother would handle any pack business that might crop up. Dad didn't need to know the details. He was too cranky.

After breakfast and lots of idle chitchat, I loaded the dishwasher. Skye rinsed and handed me the dishes. Working together like this was amazing. We'd taken care of patients with each other at the hospital, but after the night we'd had, I felt so connected to her. I couldn't imagine how much better it might feel after we'd completely bonded.

When I finished wiping the counters, I turned to Skye. "I'm going to take a quick shower, then we'll head to your house so you can change?" I asked.

She nodded and smiled, so I turned to leave the room.

"Don't start the dishwasher yet," I told her as I backed out of the kitchen. "We can start it before we leave."

Skye simply smiled back at me as I turned and headed for the bathroom. I turned the water up as hot as I could stand it, trying to rush through my routine in case she needed a shower as well. After the previous night, she probably would.

Thinking about it again had my dick waking up. She hadn't complained, but I knew I'd been kind of rough with her in my eagerness to have her. There was a possibility she'd be too sore for more, even if we had time this morning. I lathered up my hand, gripped my hard length, and started pumping, intending to relieve myself quickly.

Then the shower curtain rustled behind me. "I see you've gotten yourself ready for me," Skye said in a purring voice.

Her fingers slid across my slick back, and I slowed my hand. She wrapped her arms around my waist, pressed her naked body against me, and removed my hand to replace it with hers. I leaned against the shower wall with one hand, trying to hold myself back. This woman was going to be the death of me.

"Show me how you like it," she whispered.

A shiver ran down my spine, despite the heat of the water crashing down over us. I took her hand, clamped down harder, and did as she asked. The soap rinsed off, but that didn't matter so much. Skye knew what she was doing.

She grabbed my shoulder and spun me, pressing my back to the wall, and kept going. In seconds, the rest of the soap had rinsed off and it was just her hand and my dick. At least until she got down on her knees.

I groaned out loud when she took me into her mouth. My hands automatically went to her hair, the brown turning nearly black under the water. Seeing her in that prone position made me want to dominate her as I had in bed. I wanted to fuck her mouth, feel the back of her throat, force her to swallow me.

It was testing my restraint, but I stopped myself and let her take the lead. Part of her liked it, I could tell, but I didn't want to test her too quickly and scare her off. Besides, she knew what she was doing.

Skye used her hand in coordination with her mouth so that all of me was covered. Her tongue was creating the most delectable sucking action that I was afraid I'd come too soon. No, damn, I was going to.

"Skye, I'm about to—"

She sat back, licking the tip one last time, then pumped hard with her hand the way I'd shown her. Her other hand, I'd noticed, was between her own legs. Pressure built up and up and then let go all over her. She moaned as my seed splashed across her breasts, and damn if that didn't make an erotic sight.

The water washed it away soon enough, but the image would stay with me forever.

I pulled her to her feet and slid my fingers where hers had been moments ago. She grabbed my face and plunged her tongue into my mouth. Spinning us, I pressed her against the wall. My fingers spun rapidly around her clit, eliciting whimpers from her as our tongues danced.

"Are you ready for me?" I whispered in her ear. I was already recovered, something I'd gathered over the years wasn't a human capability. Perks of being a dragon.

Her lust-filled gaze met mine, pupils dilated, and she lifted one leg to my hip. "Please."

I didn't need to be told twice. She wanted me as badly as I did her. Grabbing her leg, I bent my knees and eased myself into her. The shower might've helped a bit, but she was so wet and warm and perfect. I pressed my forehead to hers as she gasped, but her expression was one of elation rather than pain as I'd expected.

Taking the opportunity to show off my strength, I grabbed her other leg and lifted her off of the shower floor. She wrapped her arms around my neck and grinned.

Leaning in, she whispered against my lips. "Give it to me hard and fast."

If I hadn't had so much self-control, I would've finished again just at those words. She liked it rough. I could give that to her. I took her mouth hungrily, letting myself go the way she wanted.

Slamming into her mercilessly, I held nothing back. Her legs were looped over my arms, back pressed against the slick wall, and the angle was utter perfection. Skye's face lit up in sheer ecstasy as I repeatedly hit that sensitive spot deep inside. Her wild moans were louder in the relatively small space, and it only served to drive me on.

We were going to get a late start to our day, but I didn't care. Everything I wanted was right there in front of me, riding me, driving me crazy with need. I'd be surprised if I ever saw her at work and didn't jump her in the nearest utility closet. All I wanted to do now, all day, every day, was her.

She bit down on my bottom lip, the sharp sting of it zipping to my core, driving another orgasm closer to the surface. The feeling of her teeth in my flesh made me think of claiming her, but it was way too soon for that. Still, the urge drove me into her harder until she was breathless. I wanted to bite her so much it made my gums tingle, but I managed to hold myself back.

Her insides clamped down hard around me as she came and I kept up my rhythm, the friction pulling me along with her until I could barely stand. I grunted as I came hard, filling Skye, giving her everything I had. After a minute, I pulled out and gently set my mate down. Her legs were wobbly but held on, and I pressed her to the wall again and just kissed the woman I was going to spend the rest of my life with.

The water was starting to lose some heat by then, so I shut it off.

"You," she breathed, "are something else."

We didn't make it out of the house until much later in the morning than I'd intended to.

Not that I minded.

We held hands out to the car, and for some reason, we didn't talk much on the drive to her house, but it was okay. It was comfortable. Like we were getting used to being with one another without the pressure of conversation.

"I won't be five minutes," Skye said when I parked in her driveway.

"Dress comfortably and wear running shoes," I called out the window.

She turned and walked backward and saluted me.

Once she was back in the car, I stopped at a convenience store to grab a few snacks. I'd brought a couple of full water bottles from home. Skye's face relaxed into more of a grin as I got closer to our destination. She knew where I was headed.

"I stopped coming after you left," she whispered when I parked at the trailhead. "The memories were too painful."

My heart fell. This had been a huge mistake. "I understand. It's something else I took from you. Would you like to go somewhere else?"

"No," she exclaimed. "I'm so happy to hike this with you again."

I loaded up the backpack and wouldn't let her carry anything. What was the point of being a dragon if I couldn't handle a little extra weight?

The trail was narrow and most of the way she hiked in front of me. It wasn't conducive for talking, so I let myself reconnect with nature as we moved.

The few times the trail widened, we talked about this and that. She seemed a little shy, looking at me out of the corner of her eye.

"What is it?" I asked.

"I'm curious about your dating life." She had to walk in front of me for a bit, so I had time to gather my thoughts, but she continued her question. "I'm sure you weren't a prude, but did you have any serious relationships?"

I was completely honest with her. "I've dated a few women." Maybe not completely honest. I could've told her they were female dragons that were in the area. "I never settled down."

"Why?"

"They weren't you," I said simply and honestly. "I would've been settling."

She tried to hide her smile, but my chest puffed out, my dragon pleased that she was happy by my answer. Hell, it was true.

"Tell me more about Bret?" I partly didn't want to know. Whatever it was would likely make me hate the bastard even more.

"Um, I'm not totally sure what you already know. We met in college. He seemed perfect, proposed, the whole nine yards. I fell for him hook, line, and sinker. Then, a few months out from the wedding, he gets someone else pregnant." She shrugged and pulled ahead and finished telling me again when the trail widened. "He used our wedding date and plans to marry her. She's due any day now. And I'm happy to be away from him. I hadn't realized what a narcissist he was. I guess I was in too deep, but he and I together were the height of unhealthy."

I thanked my lucky stars that he'd gotten someone else pregnant. Not that I would've ever in a million years wished that pain on Skye. But if Bret hadn't cheated, or rather if he hadn't gotten caught, she might've been with him when I moved home.

Talk about torture. "Well, I'm sorry you were hurt in the process, but I'm so glad you're not with him anymore."

She reached over and took my hand. "Me, too," she whispered. "It wouldn't be so bad if it weren't for the pregnancy. Made me feel like such a fool. And I had no idea."

"Yeah." I sighed. "That part sucks and makes me want to rip him limb from limb. But it's his loss and my gain."

We reached the falls, the highlight of the trail, and where we'd always turned back. After sitting in front of the tall, impressive waterfalls and eating our snacks, we headed back down. As soon as I had service again, near the end of the trail, I got on my phone and texted Jace. He'd agreed to do me a favor, I just had to tell him when.

"What now?" Skye asked as we got back in the car.

"Well, I've got one more thing up my sleeve. It doesn't start until dark, could I interest you in a quick dinner?"

Our hike had taken most of the day and the snack hadn't gone far for me, and Skye nodded her head vigorously. "Yes, please. I'm starving."

"Excellent. Actually, I think I can incorporate our dinner into our evening plans. Is that okay?"

She shrugged. "Since I don't know what it is, I'll say yes."

Chuckling, I told Skye about my first roommate in Boston, a disastrous guy who had a goldfish that had died. By the time I got to the chicken restaurant, I had her rolling with laughter. Before I'd gotten him out of my apartment, he'd accused me of killing his goldfish, and I'd woken up in the middle of the night to find him staring at me.

We parked at the town square, where a movie was being screened with a projector. Jace had sent someone to sit here and save us a spot on the grass. I burst out laughing as I walked up. Jace was here, and he'd brought a picnic.

"I thought you said to bring dinner," he cried.

"Oh, no," Skye said. "I'm starving, I'm sure I can eat both."

Jace gave me a dark look. "I cooked this myself."

"Here." I thrust the bag of chicken toward him. "You have this for dinner. We'll have this delicious spread you've made for us." Whatever it was.

"Did you get extra crispy?" Jace asked suspiciously.

Skye, with her head already in the picnic basket, snorted. "Is there any other kind?"

Jace grinned down at her. "I like her." He snatched the bag of chicken from me and took off. "Have fun!" he called.

"You're a sap," Skye said as she pulled out containers and spread them out on the blanket. "I would've been fine with subs and a six-pack."

Settling down beside her, I laughed and leaned in for a kiss in front of everyone at the town square. Several of the people here were definitely in my clan.

She held out her face and allowed me to press a slow, lingering kiss to her lips. "I'm glad you never let that side of you go. Sometimes subs and beer are just what the doctor ordered, but for tonight, we have…" I peered into one of the containers. "Whatever the hell this is."

"I think it's soup," she said. "I'm cooled off enough now that it sounds pretty yummy, too."

I pulled out an inflatable pool float thing from the bottom of the picnic basket. "Nice touch, Jace," I murmured. After we finished eating, I spent several minutes blowing it up, then settled down on it and wrapped the blanket around my shoulders.

Skye snuggled in beside me, both of us barely fitting. As the movie came on, I inhaled her scent and closed my eyes, totally ignoring the movie as my tattoo tingled on my arm. It didn't burn, it almost tickled. Surely that meant progress.

We snuggled through the movie, and when it was over packed everything up and walked back to the car.

As time drew nearer for me to tell her the truth, the more I wanted to back out. It was too soon. Telling her the truth now would've just made her run screaming. I couldn't let that happen. I had to give it more time. Today had been idyllic and almost perfect. Did I really want to ruin that now? Did I want to risk the relationship we were building? I had to be sure, *damn* sure that she was just as in love with me as I already was with her. I wasn't ready. She wasn't ready. It wasn't time. Just a little while longer. Just a little while.

Chapter 15 - Skylar

Sighing, I munched on my carrot stick and tried not to feel all melancholy. Anthony and I hadn't had sex again since that first night and that was *three* weeks ago. Three! What in the hell? When a day had dragged to two and then more and more, and one week turned to two and then three, my doubts turned into full-blown paranoia. I had to have done something wrong. We'd had a great day the next day. He'd wined and dined me, and then Monday when we went to work, things went south.

Even though we'd had a few more dates since then, the fireworks hadn't gone off again. Not like the night I showed up on his front porch. So, what? Was it not good for him? I brushed that thought away because he'd clearly enjoyed himself. But I still couldn't figure out why we hadn't had sex again.

It wasn't for lack of me wanting to, because *hot* damn, I did. I reminded myself that we'd been working alternating schedules at the hospital. When he was off work, I was on. It had been his weekend to work, then mine the weekend after. Most of the reasons we'd been apart hadn't been anyone's fault. One of the days I'd asked if he could go out, he'd promised his parents he'd have dinner with them, and then another time that he'd asked me, I'd promised Dad and Cooter I'd come for dinner.

Even after the two dates, though, it had been Anthony who had shut down the prospect of sex. Both times. It was like he was scared of it.

What the hell? Not that sex was all I cared about, but I'd been going through a very dry spell since Bret had done what he did, and my time with Anthony was like a damn dam had broken loose. I felt like I should've been carrying a wet floor sign around with me. My libido needed to calm the hell down and let me enjoy the other perks of having a man court me.

As I sat in the cafe eating area, I looked around, trying to figure out what was off about the day. It was like something buzzing in the air. I couldn't quite put my finger on it, but my skin was electrified. Whatever it was, it didn't feel natural.

Was there such a thing as excess electricity in the air? I didn't want to ask anyone else in case it was nothing more than me being totally nucking futs.

I'd never experienced anything like this before and it made me feel crazier and crazier as the day wore on. I carried on throughout the day, and it was one of those days that Anthony had off during the week because he'd picked up a weekend day. I missed seeing him, but the distraction of the strange buzzing electricity distracted me from it.

A little while after lunch, Anthony walked in as I traded out my dead tablet for one with a fresh battery at the nurses' station. I raised my eyebrow and tried not to look overly pleased to see him. We'd agreed to keep any forms of PDA to a minimum at work.

It was hard to wipe the smile off my face though. As soon as he spotted me, he headed my way. He looked different somehow, and it wasn't the new-boyfriend haze. I was sure I saw him through rose-colored glasses, but this wasn't that.

Something in his walk made me pay attention to him, as if the way he moved forced me to acknowledge him, forced me to *see* him.

His lip curled as if he was pleased. "What do you have planned tonight?"

"Nothing, I thought about going to Dad's, but I never told him that I was coming."

He nodded and looked even more pleased with himself or maybe me. "I'm glad to hear it. I've got something I really need to talk to you about. Can you come to my place?"

My emotions went a little wild. First, I remembered the last time I went to his house, which had been a fun night. Then, I grew concerned, more like an instant moment of panic, about what he could want to talk about. After the absent three weeks we'd had, I couldn't help but be apprehensive.

"It's nothing for you to worry about." He opened his mouth to say something else, but just then, Cam walked up, and he clamped his lips shut.

He might not have thought I needed to worry, but I couldn't fully trust it.

He greeted Cam warmly but waited for her to walk away to speak to me again. "I'm sorry I can't pick you up, but do you think you could be there around eight?"

I nodded dumbly. That was so, so many hours from now. Hours for me to finish work and then go home and worry. Great.

Anthony looked around and when he saw nobody was in the vicinity, he leaned over and pecked a quick kiss to my forehead before turning to leave.

Confused, intrigued, and skeptical, I grabbed my fresh tablet and headed to my next appointment.

As I suspected, I spent the rest of the afternoon worrying. Then, I went home and did every bit of primping that I could think of, from painting my nails to plucking my eyebrows to neatening up *down there.*

I spent extra time in the shower shaving my legs, lotioned every inch of my body, and did my hair and makeup perfectly.

Dressing was harder. Was I going to get lucky? Ugh.

Probably not. But just in case, I put on my favorite lingerie.

As I pulled the lacy panties up, I couldn't help but wonder

what kind of lingerie Anthony liked. Not knowing

unnerved me a little. What if he was a sweet sort of guy?

All pale pinks and flowers? Because I'd have to go

shopping if that was the case. I didn't own a damn thing

that was sweet. Everything in my lingerie drawer was sexy

and sensual. Bold colors, sheer fabrics.

Oh, well. If I found out he liked softer things, I guessed that

was my excuse to hit up the lingerie store. For now, a black

set would do the trick either way. Who didn't like black

lingerie? Nobody.

Arguing with myself over lingerie wasted an entire five

minutes, but it was still an hour too early to leave. I wasted

more time picking out an outfit, and then once I was as

fixed up as it was possible to be, I sat on the couch and

played on my phone and pretended I wasn't checking the

clock every thirty-five seconds. As I played a mindless game, I came up with a million scenarios as to what Anthony was up to and each scenario was crazier than the last. I finally got control of myself and got my brain to shut down from the crazy before I readied myself to head over to his place.

Everything is fine.

I repeated the phrase over and over as I drove toward Anthony's place, but that strange energy I felt earlier pulsated around me. It made me feel nauseated and was so overwhelming.

I had to pull the car over for a moment at the end of Anthony's long driveway, near his parents' house, and catch my breath.

I rolled down the window and gulped in the still cool early spring air, and as a light breeze tickled past my ear, I could've sworn I heard Anthony whisper that everything was okay. In the back of my mind, the words flashed that I was safe, but that couldn't have been right. The buzzing intensified. I was losing my damn mind!

Whatever it was, I had to get there and tell him about it. It had escalated to causing physical symptoms. I needed a diagnostician, but I knew what it had to be. It was a brain tumor. That was the only explanation.

I got to Anthony's place in one piece, and when I got out of the car, it felt like I was going to be blown over, but there was no wind to speak of. The breeze was light and cooled my cheeks, yet it didn't seem like I was imagining things as I reacted to the pulsing energy in the air.

It became like a trail, drawing me forward. I didn't know what compelled me to follow it, but my instinct told me to let it guide me.

Fear blossomed and my hands shook. What was happening? I followed the pull and it led me around

Anthony's house. There was a small path in the trees and short candles lit the track. I followed them with my stomach nearly heaving as the buzzing reached critical levels. Eventually, I stumbled into a clearing.

Anthony stood in the center with moonlight shining down on him. He looked ethereal and I didn't know how I knew but suddenly I was certain that nothing would ever be the same. My life was about to change, for better or worse, out here in the woods on a cool spring night.

Anthony gestured for me to come to him. I looked around, apprehensive, and having a hard time ignoring all the physical symptoms I'd been feeling. But still, my instincts told me to move, so I moved.

Smiling, with a lot of emotion in his eyes, Anthony took my hands. His skin was warmer than normal, but I'd noticed that a few times. He seemed to run a little hot. Unusual, but not unheard of. My body was still acting crazy, but I wasn't afraid. Yet something was definitely off. "Anthony," I whispered. "What's going on?"

Then it hit me. "Oh, no." I moaned and tried to pull my hand from his. "Are you guys really a cult? Is this some sort of initiation?" Scenarios for what Anthony might try to do to me to initiate me into his cult ran through my head and none of them were comforting at all.

Anthony laughed and swung my hands. "We aren't a cult, but we are something… more."

Damn it. All these years I'd defended them. And here it was down to the wire, and I was about to be inducted into a cult.

Anthony leaned in and met my gaze. He was so serious with so much emotion in his eyes. "I need you to understand that I'd never harm you. Hurting you goes against everything you are to me."

I laughed, not scared but getting nervous. "Why would I think you'd hurt me?"

"Soul mates are real, Skylar."

That was a conversation we could have, but not in the woods behind his house at dusk. "Okay, well—"

"For my kind, it's a lot stronger."

I stiffened and tried to pull my hands back again. "What the hell are you talking about? Anthony, you sound crazy. Your kind?"

"Don't be afraid. But there's more to the world around you than you could imagine." He lowered his eyes guiltily. "I haven't been honest with you, but it was for the safety of me and my people." My heart beat hard in my chest. The insane electricity intensified. "I can't keep it a secret anymore because our relationship is progressing and there are things that must happen but *can't* happen if you don't understand who I am, *what* I am, and what you are to me."

My stomach clenched painfully as my adrenaline spiked. My fight-or-flight instinct kicked in. "Anthony," I said warningly. I was about to take the hell off.

"I am the alpha of the Bluewater Coast Clan."

Alpha of the who now?

He pulled back his sleeve, and I gasped when I saw he'd gotten a massive tattoo. It was of a dragon and went from his wrist to his inner elbow and wrapped around to the outside of his arm. The tattoo seemed to be glowing.

No way. Could he mean—? No. No way. None of this made any sense. It was completely unreal. I stared at Anthony, and he let out a deep breath. "When did you get a tattoo?" I asked weakly.

"Skye," he said gently. "It's not a tattoo, not really. It's a mark that appears when I find my mate. And you couldn't see it until I told you about it and even then, you'd only be able to see it if some part of you believed in it. I'm a dragon. My family… We're dragons."

Chapter 16 - Anthony

The silence pretty much deafened me as I waited for Skye to respond to my admission. Her heart was about to beat out of her chest. I heard it across the few feet that separated us. She was either nervous or scared. I didn't smell fear, so probably just a lot of confusion.

"Do you think this is a joke?" Oh, damn. She sounded upset.

"No, I'm not joking."

She backed up and shook her head. "Why are you doing this? Is this your way of pushing me away without having to be open and honest with me?"

Oh, damn it. I'd done it wrong. She thought I was trying to pull one over on her. "No, Skye, no." I threw my hands up, but when I moved toward her, she pulled away. "I'm not joking. I don't want to push you away. I want to get closer to you. The *last* thing I want is to push you away."

She scrunched up her shoulders. "I don't know, you sound like a lunatic." Her gaze darted around the clearing, locating the trail she'd come in on.

"Wait…" I backed up, giving her space to not feel so overwhelmed. "Let me just show you. But promise me, no matter what happens, *promise* you'll remember I won't hurt you."

She furrowed her brow. "I don't believe you'd hurt me."

Relief washed over me. "Okay, just keep repeating that." As I moved farther into the clearing, I smiled at her and then called on my dragon to initiate the shift.

In the midst of the change, I heard her gasp. A tang of fear filled the air. It was easy to smell once my nose shifted. I finished my shift and opened my eyes. Skylar was pale and her eyes wide. She had one hand covering her mouth.

I was sure she was going to run, but she didn't. Her heart was racing so loud it thumped a rhythm against my eardrums.

"Am I dreaming?" she said in a breathy voice.

I shook my large head. I'd projected my thoughts to her earlier, but I wasn't sure if she'd heard me since she wasn't a dragon. But I'd hoped that since she was my mate, it might work. *You're not dreaming.*

She didn't react at first, so I assumed it didn't work. Disappointment washed over me. If I'd been able to talk to her, it would've been further proof that we had a true and real connection. I believed we did, but it would help convince my clan if she heard me.

"Did you just talk in my head?" Her voice sounded weak and suddenly I worried she was going to pass out.

I wanted to rush forward, but having a full-grown dragon rushing at her might not have been the best idea. *Only the alpha of each clan can communicate with his clan this way.*

She stepped forward a few feet but stopped well short of me. "Is this real?" She'd dropped to a whisper again.

I remained very still as she kept inching forward, and when I spoke in her head again, I tried to speak softly, but it wasn't like talking out loud. It wasn't an exact science. Hell, it wasn't a science at all. It was pure magic. *This is all too real. You're in no danger, and I'm really a dragon.*

She jumped and giggled, and I thanked my lucky stars because some of the tension in the air thinned. She scoffed and then sighed, the emotions bouncing off of her changing at lightning speed. "At least a lot of things make more sense to me now. Like why everyone in town thinks you guys are a cult. In a way, you are." She cocked her head when I spoke again.

We're trying to protect ourselves from people finding out, but it makes us seem weird.

She stepped forward again, nearly close enough to touch me now. "So, why are you telling me?" she asked.

I wasn't sure I wanted to be in my dragon form for the fated mates conversation. *I'll tell you all about that when I'm on two legs again.*

She nodded. "Fair enough." Her shuddering breath ran through me. Now that she was settling and knew she wasn't in danger, that this was still me, she was growing more excited. I waited patiently for her to move toward me.

Her hand shook a little, and the mischievous side of me considered chuffing at her because it would've made her jump and squeal, but I stayed perfectly still. There was plenty of time to tease her later in life. For now, I needed her to accept me and get more comfortable with the fact that the world as she knew it had changed.

What felt like an eternity later, her hand rested on my nose. Electricity sizzled between us and she giggled low in her throat.

"Does it hurt when you shift?" she asked as she began to walk slowly around me.

No.

"Well, how does it happen?"

Magic. I didn't clarify. Not yet.

"Oh, like a witch casts a spell on you?" she asked derisively.

I didn't answer, because it was a lot like that. Sammy's ancestor had invented a spell that made it possible for us to shift painlessly and Sammy had come up with a genius solution to our clothing. She did something to us during our initial shift that made our clothes sort of hang out in limbo so that when we shifted back, there they were, good as new. It caused a slight drain to our energy, but not enough for any of us to even notice anymore.

She walked around my other side and looked me in the eye. "Are witches real?"

Every clan has a witch. Traditionally, the dragons provided the witch protection. Nowadays, we just pay her. It's her full-time job to help the clan.

Her jaw slackened enough for her mouth to open a little. She breathed out with wide eyes. I could practically hear her mind racing. "Does the witch brainwash people?"

That was a more complicated answer. I stepped toward her, eager for her to continue exploring my large body.

"Got it," she said. "We'll have to talk more about that, too. That seems terribly violating." I nuzzled her arm and looked up at her. "Stretch out," she said. "I want to see how big you are. You've been trying to look small, haven't you?"

It was true. I'd hunched down as much as I could, trying to seem unintimidating. Standing at my full height, I stretched out my neck and tail and puffed out my chest, proud to show her my impressive size. I was the biggest member of our clan, as alphas tended to be.

She gasped in wonder when she saw me. "Can you breathe fire?" she asked.

Our clan are water dragons. I can manipulate water and breathe it out the way the dragons of human lore can do fire.

"Okay," she said. "I admit, that's pretty cool."

She continued on with her questions. "What about lifespan?"

We live the same lifespans as humans, but we tend to live to the max of those years. The oldest dragon in my memory was a hundred and five, but most live to their nineties.

"Illness? Surgeries?" As she asked, she circled me, and I knew her medically trained eyes were taking in my physique, my skin, scales, and in her mind, she was picturing my circulatory systems and trying to figure out how I shifted.

It's magic. You won't find a scientific reason for this. At least not one that we've discovered yet. If science was behind this, it was a science far, far beyond human reckoning or understanding. *And no, we generally don't get diseases, or if we do, we almost always recover. We can still get the occasional cold, but it's milder than a human.*

She ran out of steam after asking a few more questions and circling me several more times. "You've got a lot of explaining to do," she said and crossed her arms.

I shifted back, my clothes perfectly in place as if I'd never even moved.

She shivered. "I'm not sure I'll get used to that."

Holding out my hand, I prayed she'd take it, meaning she was open to all of this. Anything but a full rejection I could handle. She hesitated but took my hand. We walked back down the trail toward my house, and she kept her distance, our arms outstretched between us. I understood. This shit was crazy. I grew up with it, and still sometimes felt like it was beyond comprehension.

I walked in my back door which opened into my kitchen. "Here," I said. "You need a glass of wine." She started to protest, but I chuckled. "After what you just saw, don't you think you deserve it?"

With a snort, she hopped up onto the chair at my kitchen island. "Okay, when you put it that way, I guess so."

A few minutes later, Skye sipped at the red wine and sucked in a deep breath. "So, why did you think I deserved to know about this enormous secret?"

And here was the second half of the enormous secrets I had to give up today. I gulped down several ounces of my wine. "Do you still like to read?" I asked. I'd gone over how to tell her this part over and over. When we were kids, she'd loved to read, and I knew from the women in the clan talking that romance novels often got it pretty right.

She gave me a confused look. "Yeah, what's that got to do with anything?"

"According to the female dragons I know—"

"Wait," she interrupted. "Women are dragons too?"

I raised my eyebrows. "Why wouldn't they be?"

Her mouth opened and closed at me. "I don't know. I guess I have read too many shifter books where it's only the men who are shifters."

I nodded encouragingly. "So, what do those books say about fated mates?"

Her eyes widened. "You're not saying what I think you're saying."

Oh, yeah. She was getting it. I grinned at her while I waited for her to get there.

"I'm your fated mate?" she asked. Her face was so shocked I wasn't sure if she was glad to hear it or dismayed.

"I always had feelings for you. When we were kids, they were innocent, but as we got older, they morphed into more. Something deeper. And then I finally decided to do something, and I kissed you." Holding out my arm, I showed her my tattoo again. "This is the mark. When a male dragon discovers his fated dragon mate, he develops a tattoo that burns onto his skin. It's actually pretty painful."

"And the woman?" she asked.

"Female dragons' tattoos develop as their feelings for their mate grow. Slower, and less painfully."

"Dragons?" she asked.

And the last hard thing to tell her. "That's the thing. That's what's made all this so difficult. As far as any of us know, there's never been an instance of a dragon mating with a human. It's why my parents freaked out. It's why they sent me away and why I was afraid to contact you."

She snatched up her wine glass and gulped down the contents. "Never?"

I shrugged. "While I was away, I researched all over the world. Took trips. Asked *everyone*. If it's happened before, nobody is willing to admit to it." I reached across the kitchen island and put my hand on hers. "And some people aren't too happy about it."

"At least you leaving makes more sense now," she said. "Because I tried to accept it before, but it never made any sense. It was so out of character and out of what I ever would've expected from you."

I squeezed her hand. "But you should know that before the tattoo ever showed up, I'd decided I wanted to take you for my chosen mate. We have a choice. The tattoo has never shown up on someone in love and committed to another woman. And I loved you. I never stopped. I've loved you since I was old enough to know what it meant."

She looked at me with big, watery eyes, then turned her hand over underneath mine so that we held each other's hands. "What does it mean to be a mate to a dragon?"

I smiled, thrilled she was asking questions as if she was accepting this. "It's not really more than being married and committed to one another. The magic just recognizes that we're especially compatible and most likely to achieve lifelong happiness. Have you ever felt pulled toward me?"

She ducked her head. "As long as I've known you. I just always figured we had a connection, not *the* connection."

I chuckled and circled around the island to stand close to my mate. "Our connection is growing."

She gasped. "Since this morning, I've felt like my skin was electrified. It overwhelmed me. I nearly threw up!"

"Once it's sealed, it's like we're married in the eyes of the magic."

"Sealed?" She raised her eyebrows. She probably had an idea what I meant, thanks to those books she liked to read. "What does that entail?"

"It's a bite," I admitted.

She snorted. "Will I turn into a dragon?"

I started to say no, but then I realized I had no idea. "That's something I can't answer. There is no precedence for this. As I said, I wasn't able to find other instances of human mates, male or female."

She nodded. "Well, we can figure that out. Maybe your witch will have some answers." Her arched eyebrow told me she was teasing me about having a witch.

I chuckled. "Would you like to stay with me?" I asked.

She hesitated and looked around the room before meeting my gaze again. "Yes. I would."

Thank fuck.

Chapter 17 - Skylar

"Let's go sit down and get comfortable," Anthony suggested.

My heart was full of love but also still pretty damn shocked. Everything felt surreal. I should've been more upset or shell-shocked, but I kept my composure. It was easier to keep it than I would've expected. Even with the fear of the unknown, I knew one thing for certain and that was that Anthony had always been my person. With that in mind, my stress left. He was my person, and I was even more sure of it now with the whole fated mate situation.

We had barely settled in the living room with our wine glasses replenished when his doorbell rang. He sat straight up. "Damn. I'm so distracted. I normally hear people drive up."

He set his glass on the coffee table and jogged to the door. When he opened it, his father's gaze pinned on me. They'd known I was in here. Well, they probably saw my car.

"What are you guys doing here?" Anthony asked.

"Darling, we *felt*," his mother raised her eyebrows warningly, "as if you needed some assistance."

He chuckled. "I was afraid of that. Come in. She knows."

His mother's jaw dropped. "She does?" She turned to her husband. "See, Mitch? I told you she wouldn't run screaming." She walked into the room carrying what looked suspiciously like a casserole wrapped in a towel. "I brought dinner."

She hurried through the house. "Don't bother!" She waved Anthony off as he tried to follow her. "I've got it. I'll just put it in the oven on warm."

"That was nice of you," I said, feeling more timid than I'd felt since I was sixteen. But then, these were the people who made Anthony leave.

Mitch glared at me and plopped down in one of Anthony's recliners. His living room was quite big, which was nice. Mine was cozier, but it was right on the beach.

Karah returned from the kitchen with a beer in one hand and another glass of wine in the other. "Hope you don't mind if we join you," she said in a chirpy voice.

Mitch rolled his eyes, but she shoved the beer in his hands. "Drink, Mitch," she said darkly.

It was all I could do not to laugh as he gave her a sullen look and did as he was told. I assumed he'd been the alpha before Anthony. Big bad dragon alpha, doing exactly as his wife told him to do.

At least it set a good example for Anthony. Again, I had to force myself not to giggle.

Anthony put his arm around me in a gesture of solidarity. "She did amazingly," he said. "I couldn't have asked for her to handle the news better. We won't need Sammy after all." So they knew he was telling me, and had the witch on standby. To what, wipe my memory? What the hell.

Karah beamed. "I'm so glad to hear it, dear." She perched on the arm of the chair that Mitch had settled into. Leaning forward, she patted his knee. "Mitch and I tried for more children but were only blessed with Anthony. It will be wonderful to have a daughter."

I tried not to look freaked out. My mom took off on us when I was a kid. It had taken me years to stop thinking I'd done something wrong. When I was a young woman, Dad had finally told me the full truth, that Mom had suffered from several mental illnesses like bipolar disorder. He'd been worried I would suffer the same fate, but so far so good. It had made me worried about my future children as well, but my PCOS had solved that worry.

"I can't imagine the shock of learning about the magical world this late in life." Karah shook her head, still beaming.

Mitch leaned forward and something sort of washed over me. I narrowed my eyes at him. Was he trying to use magic on me? "You can't tell anyone," he said.

"Dad, stop it." I felt the same heaviness in Anthony's voice. They were using magic! "She knows she can't blab. And don't use your leftover alpha powers on my mate."

Mitch sat back and looked extraordinarily grumpy. "As the previous alpha, it's my job to help keep the clan safe. As far as we know, she's the first human with permission to have this secret." He fixed me with his glare again, but this time his words didn't carry the same weight. "You understand there are massive consequences to revealing our secret?"

"Don't threaten my mate," Anthony said in a low, angry voice. Tension filled the air.

"Please don't argue," I said. "I do understand, but not the kind of consequences you're talking about. I imagine if I told, and you couldn't get your witch to fix it, you'd be hunted down. Studied. Researched. It would be traumatic, honestly. The drug companies alone would lock you up and study you until they found a way to make money off you."

"Exactly," Mitch said and for the first time, he didn't look completely angry. Just mostly.

"I'd never put Anthony in danger. Or the rest of you. I couldn't do that." Even though I had to wonder to myself if it was right to keep the secret of their magic when they might have the power to cure so many diseases locked in their DNA. But that wasn't my call to make. What I'd said was true. If this got out, the world would destroy them in the name of progress. "It's not my secret to tell."

Karah looked convinced, but Mitch still looked skeptical. I didn't care, though. I just had to prove it to them.

I slept fitfully, at least until Anthony came to bed and wrapped his arms around me. When I got up the next morning, though, he was downstairs. At least it gave me some time to take a shower and think about things.

I let the hot water run down my back and ran the events of my life through my head. I assessed my emotions and anxiety.

Now that I'd slept on it, I wasn't so freaked out. Interesting. I mean, of course I was, a little. He was a *dragon,* after all. But even with the fear of the unknown, this wasn't something I was willing to walk away from. As I lathered up my hair, I thought about how much it had hurt for him to leave. Could I survive that if he did it again?

He seemed pretty grounded here now. I didn't know clan or dragon politics very much, but it seemed like it wouldn't be the best idea for an alpha to leave his clan. Unless the whole lot of them packed up and took off, and that really didn't seem likely.

I grabbed Anthony's showerhead and put it on pulse to rinse off. When I turned it toward my groin area, the water pulsed against my clit and I gasped. My water pressure sucked, and I never had the opportunity to get off that way.

But why do it here, now? Anthony was downstairs. We were alone in the middle of the woods, and I'd all but decided I wanted to take this thing all the way. I finished rinsing off and jumped out, then brushed my teeth and wrapped myself in one of his big, fluffy towels and my hair in another.

Instead of going back into his bedroom to dress, I walked

downstairs. He wasn't in the kitchen or living room, but the

front door was cracked open just a hair.

Throwing the towel off of my hair, I shook it out around

my shoulders and pinched my cheeks for a little color.

Then, I opened the front door and leaned against the frame.

"I'm done freaking out," I said in my sultriest voice.

Bingo. Anthony's pupils widened. I was about to get

exactly what I wanted.

Chapter 18 - Anthony

The next morning, we both had to work, so I set the alarm extra early. I'd never tried to get ready with a woman in the house. Who knew how long it would take? Skye showered first while I sat on the front porch and drank a cup of coffee.

I heard her coming down the stairs, and when she opened the door, she wore a towel and nothing else. "I'm done freaking out," she said.

I laughed and held out my hands to take hers. "You're entitled to it. I'm surprised at just how well you handled all this." I pulled her close. "How are you really feeling?"

"It's all a shock but at the end of it all, you're still Anthony. No matter *what* you are, you've never been anything but Anthony to me."

I stared at her for a long time before speaking. "You really mean that?"

She nodded with her gaze full of emotion and I knew she did mean it. Skye's damp hair was sexy as hell and knowing that there was nothing under that towel was killing me. She bit her bottom lip, tilting her head so that her emerald eyes sparkled in the predawn light. I leaned forward slowly and pressed my lips to hers. She opened her mouth in invitation, and I didn't hesitate.

I scooped her up and carried her inside, pressing her against a wall just inside the door. Her arms wrapped around my neck; legs hooked around my hips. When I pressed flush against her, I could feel the heat of her core through my pants. My rapidly stiffening cock rebelled against its restraint.

Though, as badly as I wanted her, I also wanted to slow down and take my time. Every part of me longed for her, wanted to bite her, make her mine. I needed to control myself, lest I end up doing something she wasn't ready for. Not to mention we had to be at work in a short hour.

Adjusting my grip on her thighs, I carried her through the house, up the stairs, and to my bed, kicking the door shut behind us. Her skin smelled like citrus and imagining her using my body wash in my shower awoke an entirely different beast. An image from the morning in the shower slammed into me and I remembered her kneeling before me, white dripping from her breasts, sliding down her stomach.

Slowly, I lowered her to the bed. Her arms loosened from my neck and she pushed her fingers into my hair, scraping her nails lightly across my scalp. A chill ran through me at that. God, but that was a feeling I didn't know I'd enjoy.

I reached for the spot where the towel tucked around itself, keeping it closed, and tugged on it until it came undone. Her body was perfection to me. Pushing the towel open further, I lavished attention all across her skin. Her nipples didn't escape notice, her slightly ticklish ribcage, the super fine fuzz on her belly, her adorable belly button. I worked my way down slowly, watching the anticipation in Skye's half-lidded gaze.

Her nails grazed my scalp again and my chest rumbled with something that would've sounded like a purr if I'd been less masculine. I cleared my throat and Skye giggled, reaching for my head again. I distracted her.

My tongue flicked across her sex, making her hiss in pleasure. Her fingers curled into the blanket instead of my hair. The taste of her was sweeter than the citrus on her skin. I could imagine getting addicted to it like a drug. She squirmed as I lapped her up, intent on getting my fill. I kept my eyes on her form, watching each muscle contraction, her beautiful breasts jiggling with each motion.

Damn, she was gorgeous.

And she was mine.

The urge to bite her pulled at me hard, to sink my teeth into her thigh right there, to see the mark of my clan on her skin. I groaned, fighting it back, but it was a near thing.

I pushed her further back on the bed, then climbed on. She looked at me, her breathing shallow and gasping, and she squeaked as I grabbed her and settled her thighs around my head. My tongue dove back in, and she fell forward to her hands. I ran my hands over her ass, massaging, spreading her cheeks, smacking one lightly.

Her hips bucked, thighs squeezing my head slightly, and the noises that she was making were music to my ears. I took the whole of her into my mouth, sucking and flicking my tongue rapidly. My hands on her ass prevented her from moving too much, but she still ground herself on my face. I was too busy enjoying every second to mind much.

I smacked her ass again, then smoothed my hand over the sting I was sure she'd felt. Her cries, her whimpers were going to be my end, but I needed to be hers first. Still, I couldn't help it when one hand slipped down my stomach and teased my cock. I gripped it hard and stroked slowly while my tongue sucked at her.

With a sharp cry, she folded in on herself, her muscles tensing and releasing as her juices flowed freely. I kept my tongue going, determined not to let anything go to waste. She heaved a few gasping breaths as she rode out her orgasm and I finally slowed, allowing her to catch her breath. My hand continued to stroke my dick and she noticed when she turned her head.

Chuckling, she crawled away from my head and down the bed. She moved my hand away and swiped her tongue across the tip before taking me wholly into her mouth. Before I could stop myself, I grabbed her head and my hips jerked. Shit, her mouth felt fantastic there.

But she didn't stay long. A few pumps and then she was straddling me.

Backward.

"Reverse cowgirl, huh?" I asked.

She gave me a sultry glance over her shoulder, grabbed me, then lowered herself down. I'd be lying if I said that her backside wasn't sexy as all hell. From the curve of her spine to her smooth cheeks that had a slight pinkness to them, courtesy of yours truly. There was so much unmarred flesh that needed a nibble—

No, dammit. My jaw hurt from clenching down on the temptation. Skye was both enticing and distracting, becoming the latter as soon as she started moving. I grabbed her hips, but she didn't need my help. She built up a rhythm all on her own, bouncing up and down, her muscles tight.

I could watch that all day, every motion she made, her damp hair sliding over her shoulders, basically using me to get herself off. Licking my lips, I smacked her ass again. If it was possible, her muscles tightened further, and I groaned in time with her.

Fuck.

Unable to take it any longer, I lurched up and grabbed her, turning so that she was on her hands and knees. She went down to an elbow, her other hand disappearing beneath her. I slid my hands along her spine, then gripped her hips and gave it to her the way she liked it.

Hard and rough.

"Anthony, yes!"

The sound of my name on her lips drove me crazy and I felt my dragon fighting for control. The need to claim her was overwhelming. I tried to focus on the physical climax that was approaching. Skye's cries urged me on, and I picked up speed, feeling the increasing tension just before release.

"Hah, yes, yes!"

Gasping with the intensity of it, I came. My seed exploded from me like a tidal wave taking out a flood wall. Skye tensed around me, and I knew she was right behind me. I thrust several more times to expel every bit of my orgasm and drag hers out as long as I could. We were both breathless, and I nearly collapsed on top of her. With my dragon behind me, I could go all day, but between fighting back the mating urge and concentrating on Skye, that had taken more out of me than I'd been prepared for. Plus, we had to get to work.

And I still wanted more.

***

I ended up picking up a surgery at the hospital late Monday afternoon, so I didn't see Skye again until Tuesday at work. And things were going great. We'd talked on the phone for a long time Monday night, to the point that I needed an extra cup of coffee on Tuesday.

I didn't bring up the bite again. She was tentatively okay with everything. The last thing I needed was to freak her out again. If we had sex, I wasn't sure what I'd do but moving too fast wasn't the answer.

When she'd had time to adjust to the fact that I wasn't completely human, then we could talk again. There was still plenty for us to figure out.

Unfortunately, I couldn't as easily put off the further conversation with my father. He texted during the workday Tuesday and asked me to stop by when I finished my shift.

I was so tired that I couldn't think of a good reason to refuse, so off to my parents' house I went. I told Skye I'd text her later. All I wanted to do was find her and cuddle up to watch a movie or something, but no, on my way to their house, I got a phone call. "Hey, Sammy, what's going on?" The clan witch didn't call me very often.

"Hey, Anthony. Sorry to bother you." She sounded uneasy.

"It's no problem at all." I spoke to my car's stereo system, since I had my phone Bluetoothed in through it. "What can I do for you?"

"As a clan witch, I'm beholden to report everything to you, the alpha."

I didn't like the sound of that. "That's how I understand it."

"Your father called and asked me to be on standby. He told me that you've revealed to a human that she's your fated mate and told her all the clan secrets. He said if it looked like she couldn't keep her word, that I'd need to step in. And he tried to get me to keep it quiet." Her voice went hushed. "I thought you should know, even though it feels a lot like tattling."

"No, you're not tattling. As you said, it was your duty to notify me. And I'm sure that if Skye tells anyone anything, you'll be called, but that will be my decision to make, not my father's."

She laughed shakily. "Okay, Anthony, thanks for taking my call."

We hung up and I continued to my parents' house, ten times angrier than I'd been before. At the last minute, I turned off of their driveway and onto mine. When I parked, I sent out a text to the clan group text that was reserved for the alpha's messages only. It was easier than trying to send a message directly into their heads like in the older days.

Clan meeting at 8:00 p.m. sharp. At the alpha's house. There will be no flying. It will be brief. It is mandatory.

Everyone knew that mandatory didn't mean call out of work or skip an appointment. It just meant everyone who could possibly come, even if it was inconvenient, should show up.

Having the meeting at eight gave people a little bit of time to get their ducks in a row, but it gave me a lot of time to stew on how pissed I was.

Instead of taking the next two hours to brood, I launched myself into the woods and shifted. It was hard to fly among the thick trees, but I managed. When the sun began to drop lower in the sky, I headed back. Just in time, too. It was a quarter to eight and people had begun to show up. My front porch was covered in members of my clan.

I walked up and greeted everyone, keeping an eye on the watch on my wrist. At exactly eight, I put one hand in the air.

My parents had just arrived, thankfully not early, which meant I hadn't had to sit there and come up with excuses for why I hadn't come by or why I was calling this meeting without talking to them about it.

"Thank you all for coming and I'm sorry to call a meeting on such short notice. As I said, I'll be brief and get to the point. I know my position as alpha can be tested, but I will not abide disrespect. Each of you has the option to openly challenge me. Going behind my back to undermine me will not be tolerated. I am ready to take this clan in a forward direction. That might mean changes. It might not, depending on the situation, but we will move as I see fit. As every alpha has before me, I have an open door. You all have opinions that I will always consider. But there will be times that I make a decision that you don't necessarily agree with."

I looked around the crowd slowly, meeting the eyes of a few people who I thought might give me more shit than others. My dad. Tessa. "That's what the clan transfers are for. If I lead the clan in a direction that you're not comfortable with, you're welcome to transfer. We even have funds set aside for those situations." We really did. It was a part of our clan emergency fund. We covered things like medical emergencies, lost wages, and large expenses if the clan member couldn't swing it. "There are options, but none of those options should be behind my back. I am your alpha." I said my last sentence with the weight of my alpha power, and the crowd collectively bowed their heads. "If there are no questions, you may go." There. I'd reminded them that if they didn't like the way I ran things, they had the option of leaving. Or they could challenge me. But I'd be damned if I was going to be cast aside by someone who wanted to do things their way.

Both of my parents stuck around. They both knew the cause of the meeting was to put my father in his place. The only reason I'd done it this way was after the conversation I'd had with Tessa. She'd glared at me the entire time and left faster than anyone else. That woman was trouble.

"Were you just trying to embarrass me?" Dad said as soon as the last car pulled out of the clearing in front of my house. "I was concerned about Skye and trying to help you out."

"Nobody knew what I said had anything to do with you, unless you told people what you did. Sammy is the only one who knew, and she's not here."

He blustered. "I'm trying to help you, son!"

"Then trust me." It was a fight not to raise my voice. Mom sighed and walked to the porch to plop down in one of the rockers. She wasn't stupid enough to think she could keep us from this argument, but I did notice her rolling her eyes a few times. "I don't understand why you're so worried about Skye," I said. "She's my mate."

Dad's shoulders slumped. "Because you're not the first, okay?"

I couldn't have been more stunned. I looked at Mom, but she was staring at Dad with a shocked expression on her face, too. "What in the hell are you talking about, Mitch?" she asked.

"I mean, you weren't the only one who looked into this. I put some feelers out that I needed resources on a, uh, touchy subject. It took some years, but I learned of a clan in Washington. One of their members realized his fated mate was human."

"How?" I exclaimed. "I contacted that clan!"

"If you'd started searching sooner, you might've found this out instead of me. You were probably in the midst of medical school when I got this information."

He was right. I hadn't contacted the Washington clan until well into my residency.

"Anyway," he said. "She was much like Skylar. Beautiful, kind, and accepting of what he was. But when he gave her the mating bite, it nearly killed her. She woke up in the hospital in hysterics and terrified of him, something in the magic didn't mix well with her blood and she became, to put it delicately, mentally distressed. When she started screaming about dragons, they took it up as her losing her mind. Their clan's witch had to come in and wipe all of her memories of him and their secrets, but the witch couldn't remove the magic from the woman's system. She was placed in a mental institution, where she remains to this day, as far as I know."

My heart plummeted. Then it rose as anger surged. "Why the hell did you wait until now to tell me this?" I yelled.

"Seriously, Mitch, this was information he needed to know. What if he already bit her?" Mom crossed her arms and glared at us.

"I was hoping it wouldn't get this far. That you'd come to your senses or that when you told her about it, she'd reject you. But this is why I asked you to come over today, to tell you. And that's why I contacted Sammy, so she'd be on standby if you gave Skye the bite and it went horribly wrong. I told her it had to do with Skye blabbing, but that wasn't it." My father stepped forward. "I'm not just thinking of you, son. I'm thinking of Skye and her well-being. What if she's like the woman in Washington? What if the bite can kill her or make her insane?" He gripped my shoulder hard. "Can you live with that? You should really rethink the mating. And maybe consider asking Sammy to remove the knowledge of the clan from Skye's mind. It won't hurt her, and she'll be safe. It's best for everyone involved if you end things with Skylar and have her memories of our secrets wiped."

There wasn't much else to say. I couldn't really refute his arguments, though his methods had been wrong. He apologized for not telling me sooner, then they left, leaving me sitting on the front porch, stunned.

Skye texted me several times, and eventually, I responded that I was worn out and headed to bed. She knew I'd had that surgery, so she was sympathetic.

I did go to bed but barely slept. When it was time to go back to work, I was in a terrible headspace. I couldn't ignore what my father had said, and it made me furious. My heart ached with every breath and I was so confused I could barely focus on my patients. Why would fate choose this for me if it weren't meant to be? What was the purpose? What was the reason?

I didn't mean to be, but I was snappy at everyone, including Skylar. She didn't have time to question me, and when I thought she might, I ducked her, including hiding in an exam room for lunch. About an hour later, she nearly bumped into me, and once again, I snapped at her. "You're being an alpha-hole," she hissed at me. "Get the stick out of your ass."

She didn't understand why I was so upset.

Her shift ended at three, but I'd picked up another surgery days ago before I knew I'd be going through all this. It wasn't a long one, but when I finished and finally headed to my car at seven, I found her sitting on the hood reading something on her phone. She didn't speak, just stared at me with one eyebrow arched.

My heart splintered when I saw her. I wanted to bawl my eyes out and tell her how sorry I was. Instead, I walked straight up to her and wrapped my arms around her. "I'm sorry," I whispered. "There's a lot going on and I'm not processing it well."

"I'm supposed to be your partner," she said into my chest. "You should talk things through with me, Anthony."

She was right, but in this case, I couldn't. How could I tell her that being with me might make her go insane? And if we had sex again, I didn't know if I could stop myself from biting her. When my dragon rode me like that, it was nearly impossible to resist. Which meant we just couldn't have sex. And I knew Skye. She wouldn't run away just from one bad case. She was a lot like me. She'd believe there had to be others and not all of them ended the same as the case in Washington. I wanted to find out more on my own and I didn't want to put that burden on her shoulders, so I decided to not tell her. "I promise I'm handling it. You don't have to worry."

She smiled uncertainly. "Okay. Promise me you'll come to me if I can help?"

I pressed a soft kiss to her lips. "Of course. Come eat dinner with me?"

We figured out over sandwiches that her girls wanted her to spend a night with them, and Jace had asked me to come by and hang out with him at the bar. We decided to spend the weekend apart. It would be good for her to wrap her mind around all this. And I needed answers. I was bound and damn determined to get them.

Chapter 19 - Skylar

Even though Anthony had acted weird as hell all week, he'd still been loving and attentive too. I decided to trust that he was going through something. I'd left it up to Bri and Kaylee to plan our girls' day. They'd done it up big and booked us the afternoon at the spa. It wasn't a night of drinking, so I was happy with it. I loved girls' time but wasn't up to partying quite as much as my best friend. Kaylee had a liver of iron.

As we sat in a mud bath, Kaylee squinted at me from behind her clay mask. "Why have you been so quiet today?"

I shrugged and patted my mask to see if it was dry yet. "No reason. Just enjoying the relaxation. I can practically feel the toxins leaching out of my skin."

"No, something else is eating at you," Bri said. We hadn't been friends all that long and already she knew me.

I sighed. "I don't kiss and tell."

Kaylee squealed and sloshed toward me in the large mud pool. "I knew there was something juicy to tell!"

"Okay, so he has basically committed himself to me. He's talking about marriage already. Picking up where we left off. The whole nine yards." I sighed and relaxed against the pillow at the back of the tub. "He's tentative and passionate. Dominating and careful of boundaries." I sighed and basked in the new relationship feeling. By the time I finished describing what he'd been like without giving up any dragon secrets or specifically describing his girth, they were swooning against the sides of the tub too.

Bri sighed. "I'm so ready. It's been long enough. I left Hayden's dad three years ago, and I want someone totally opposite from him this time. Someone sweet and attentive who doesn't party much and isn't prone to sleeping around."

I gave her a sympathetic look. "You need a homebody. Someone settled."

She nodded and sighed. "That sounds perfect." We sat in the mud for a minute. "Mostly I want someone who wants to be a father. Or even if he's got a kid or two of his own. Like a modern-day Brady Bunch." I hoped such a man existed because Bri was a catch. Any man would be beyond lucky to have her.

"Not me. I'll take the party guy that you don't want. I don't want to settle down. I'll be a fun auntie for Hayden instead, will that work?"

Bri grinned. "That sounds perfect. Then when I'm ready to cut loose, I can go hang with Auntie Kaylee."

We finished at the mud bath and headed next door in our robes for our manicures and pedicures. They settled us in incredibly comfortable massage chairs. We weren't talking much with the nail techs in the room. A woman walked in who looked very familiar. She settled into one of the chairs across from me and caught my eye several minutes later. She smiled, and her eyes turned to onyx and gold before returning to normal quickly.

She was a dragon. And still, she looked so familiar. Her smile deepened and I caught a flash of fang. Who was this woman? Her smile was nasty and in no way friendly. "Hi," she said in a haughty voice and as soon as I heard it, I knew who she was. My rideshare driver. "I'm Tessa."

"Yes, I remember you. You're…" I pursed my lips a little as I continued, letting the words roll out of my mouth as if they tasted bad. "*Friends* with Anthony, aren't you?"

She smiled again and this time I definitely saw a flash of fang. A little fear trickled through me. She breathed in deep through her nose and closed her eyes as if savoring a scent.

Oh, shit. She smelled my fear. That bitch.

"Yes," she said. "We're old friends." The way she said it was so suggestive I wanted to go over and rip her damn fangs out of her head. But fuck, I had no idea what dragons were like in their human forms. Probably, she would have kicked my ass. The hairs on my arms raised and she continued. "I've heard all about you." Her gaze dragged up and down my body as if judging every inch of me. "Apparently, people exaggerate."

I snorted. I wasn't the type to be bullied, even if she could've beat me to a pulp. "Oh, really? How odd. I've never heard of you." Of course, I had, but she didn't need to know that. I cocked my head and gave her a fake sympathetic look that was all catty. "I imagine I wouldn't if someone wasn't relevant enough for a conversation." I bit my bottom lip and wrinkled my brows, daring her to say something else.

Her face reddened. Oh, yeah. She was furious, but fuck all, I didn't care. Dragon or not, that bitch needed to know her place. I leaned forward. "It's really not becoming of a female to allow her jealousy to be so apparent. It makes you look desperate."

Tessa rose to her feet. "You're going to regret pissing me off," she said in a low, fierce voice. I did feel a little trickle of fear, but I made sure I appeared unfazed. I waved one hand at the witch and turned back to my girls, who looked shocked. Well, Kaylee looked like she was about to jump to my aid, but I wouldn't have expected less from her. When I looked back, Tessa was gone.

After the spa, we headed back to my place where we relaxed a while before heading out for a night on the town. Our dinner was spent mostly discussing Tessa.

Kaylee waved her arm as the server set chips and salsa down in front of us. "I've run into her a time or two. I don't know much about her. Just that she's super catty. But then, I don't know much about anyone in the cult."

"Please don't call them a cult. They're just a group of friends. Like us but bigger. Besides, I'm not concerned with Tessa. I'm sure if she were important, Anthony would've mentioned her." He had, but he'd told me he'd take care of her. I'd have to mention it to him that she'd been hateful again. Now that I knew she was a dragon, I disliked it all the more. But I was out with my girls, so I pushed her from my mind and enjoyed the night with my two best friends.

As the night went on, the tipsier we got. I made sure to keep it on this side of tipsy. I was in no position to be getting drunk. The longer I stayed in a slightly inebriated state of mind, the more I worried about the whole Tessa thing. And all of the rest of it. Could I really be *married* to a dragon? Could we have babies? Not that I was really concerned about that, considering my reproductive history, I'd long ago come to terms with the fact that I'd likely never carry a child of my own. But what if Anthony expected a baby? I know he'd said PCOS wasn't the end-all, but what if it turned out I definitely couldn't have one? Would he want to have one with someone else like Bret had? The doubts hit me like I was a punching bag. His parents had been concerned for a reason, what if they were right?

After we spent some time dancing, we ended up at Jace's bar. Luckily for my recovery tomorrow, I was still only slightly buzzed. Bri and Kaylee were far past the point of sober, so I decided it was best not to drink anymore that night to keep an eye on my girls. As I got them set up at the table, I looked around and spotted Tessa talking to Jace. Oh, come on. I rolled my eyes because *of course,* she was here. But then Tessa turned and there was a look on her face that screamed predator. She walked toward the stairs that led to Jace's VIP section. Something in me pushed me forward, and since the girls were giving their orders to the server, I stood. "I'll just take a soda," I told her. "Be right back." I headed toward the stairs, just buzzed enough to be courageous when probably I should've been cautious.

Chapter 20 - Anthony

The moment she walked into the bar, I felt her. I would've sensed her as soon as she was within a mile vicinity if I'd already bitten her. The fact that I knew she was in the building meant we were really close. How could the bond go so wrong in this situation? We were meant for each other.

Something tugged behind my heart. We had ended up in the same place even after saying we were going to spend the weekend apart. I was about to go downstairs to find her when Tessa appeared at the top of the stairs. Ugh. She came through the curtain divider with a triumphant look on her face. Damn it. I so wasn't in the mood to deal with her. "Excuse me," I said and tried to step aside so she could go on in and let me go out.

But she moved in the same direction I did. "I ran into your human earlier. She's got a smart freaking mouth. She's lucky I didn't claw her damn eyes out." I bristled at her threats against Skye, my alpha side wanting to put her in her place, but she kept on, ignoring the anger rolling off of me. "I just don't get how you're so hung up on her. She's weak. How are you going to be mated to someone who can't fly with you? That's going to be miserable."

I'd held my temper as long as I could. I'd never have harmed a female, but I would *always* protect my mate. I controlled myself as I advanced on Tessa. If she'd been male, this would've gone *very* differently. Pushing my alpha power in front of me like a ton of bricks, I advanced until she pressed herself against the wall and let out a whimper. Even though I could feel how cowed she was, she still looked up at me with a glint of desire in her eyes. Was she somehow *enjoying* this? Ugh. Gross. I put one hand on either side of her head and leaned close so she could see the fury in my eyes and feel the weight of my word as her alpha. "You won't threaten Skye, *ever* again. And if you know what's best for you, you'll get over your jealousy and accept that Skye isn't going anywhere."

Tessa's smile spread across her face, even though she couldn't move from the wall as I continued pressing my dominance onto her. She looked wicked, nearly evil. "Are you sure?"

"Of course I'm sure," I thundered.

Tessa looked over my shoulder and nodded her head slightly, so I'd look behind me. Skye was there, staring at both of us, and she looked positively murderous.

I turned back and read the room. Shit. From her angle, it might've looked like I had Tessa pressed against the wall for an entirely different reason. Damn Tessa for testing my patience! "Skye," I yelled. "It's not what you think."

She scoffed. "Yeah, I've never heard that one before."

Anger bubbled over inside me. I was dealing with everything from the normal pressures of being a doctor to trying to figure out how to safely mate with the woman I loved without causing her irreparable harm. Fuck! I'd been focused on research to try to help her, fighting my instincts to claim her before I was sure of her safety. Dealing with backlash from my clan members like this fucking psycho here. I didn't need her comparing me to her trash ex. "I'm not him," I yelled, turning toward her, and ignoring Tessa. "And you should give me the benefit of the doubt enough that you don't accuse me of being like him. I've been stressed and busy, but I would never do anything to hurt you. You must know that."

"Is that why you had another woman pressed against the wall with your face close enough to kiss? The same woman who told me earlier that you and she have *history*?" She edged toward the stairs again, as if ready to run back down them at any point. The VIP section wasn't large, and curtains muted the sounds of the bar below.

I turned and glared at Tessa. She shrugged, looking as unruffled as a kitten. "She deserved to know, if she's going to be part of the clan."

My frustration was at its peak, and it exploded when Tessa spoke again. "It might not matter anyway if the mating bite kills her or drives her insane."

I snarled at her. "How did you hear about that?"

She slid sideways, trying to get away from my anger, but Skye wouldn't have been able to see it. Tessa looked triumphant as she smirked at both of us and walked out of the VIP section. "Good night, you two," she said before disappearing.

Skye looked pale as she watched Tessa walk out. Through our tentative bond, I felt her fear and hurt spike. "What is she talking about?" Her small voice cut me to ribbons.

"She'll pay for her actions." I couldn't stop the venom from filling my voice. Tessa was going to learn that she couldn't do whatever she wanted to. She'd be lucky if I didn't banish her.

"Anthony," Skye yelled. "What was she talking about?"

"I can't have this discussion here," I said and rubbed my hands across my face. "Will you come home with me?"

She nodded. "Let's go."

I led her down the stairs and she headed straight for the bar, where Jace had gone to give his guy his meal break. For the most part, Jace was supposed to be off duty and hanging out with me. We'd been having a great time up in the VIP section before Tessa had ruined everything. I'd even gotten my mind off of all this bullshit for a few minutes. Then Tessa happened.

I followed Skye and listened to what she told Jace. "Please keep an eye on my girls and let them know I left with Anthony?"

Jace nodded and looked at me over her shoulder. "Sure, of course."

Skye reached leaned forward, toward my friend. "Kaylee lives right down the road." She reached into her pocket and pulled out a twenty. "Ask one of your guys to walk them down there, or if they refuse it, have them watch and make sure they get home, okay?"

Jace took the bill and looked at me again. I nodded, so he smiled at Skye. "You got it. Not a hair on their heads will be bothered."

"My house," she said when I tried to open my car door for her. She yanked it out of my hand and got in, pulling the door closed before I could. The car ride to her house was utterly silent. I almost opened my window to create a little noise. "Skye—"

"No," she said sharply. "Just don't."

When we got to her house, she jumped out of the car and marched up the walk to her front door. I followed as quickly as I could, worried that she might slam the door in my face and lock me out. But she let me in behind her, then headed straight for the kitchen.

Skye returned with a large glass of wine and paced the living room. "Start talking," she barked.

"My father told me that he'd found another instance of a male dragon biting a female human. The human went insane." Her face fell as she watched me talk.

She stopped in the middle of the living room and gulped down half the glass of wine, then paced again. "Why the fuck didn't you tell me as soon as you knew?" she said in a thunderous voice.

"Even though I'm magical, we're scientists, Skye. I couldn't bear to tell you something like this until I knew more. I couldn't lose everything, throw it all away on one story."

"Well, what the hell were you planning to do? You said you had not found any other cases of a human with a dragon. Were you going to just have Sammy wipe my memories and move on?" She snarled at me, fierce as any dragon I'd ever seen. "Move on to *Tessa*?"

"Stop it," I warned. Her head was going into a dark and spiteful place.

She carried on, of course. "That was your plan, wasn't it? Wipe my memories, then mate with Tessa. She's a dragon. She can take your bite."

She'd worked herself up into being really damn pissed. "Tell me the truth, Anthony," She practically yelled. "Were you going to wipe my memories?"

I didn't want to lie to her. I really didn't want to tell her, either. "I'd do anything to keep you safe, Skye. Not biting you is becoming harder and harder. I don't want to risk your life or your sanity. I need time to figure out if we can safely do this. If we can be together. Maybe it would be best if, until I know for sure, we stay away from each other."

I couldn't risk losing control. Not just because it was dangerous. I didn't want to bite her until she gave full consent with all knowledge of the dangers involved. "My tattoo started burning again this weekend," I said. "My dragon wants to finish this, and I don't know how long I can resist."

"Were you going to tell me?" she whispered. "Ever?"

I didn't answer.

She set her wine glass down and walked to her front door, opening it and standing beside it. "Do what you need to do," she said. "I won't fight you."

I walked over and got as close as I dared. Any closer and I'd gather her into my arms. "This isn't goodbye."

"It is if you can't find proof that I won't die or go crazy. You'll wipe my memories, even though I'd never do anything to hurt you or your family. But I guess that doesn't matter. You're alpha. You'll do what you have to do."

My heart cracked, and even though my mating bond with Skye was pulsing with my own pain, I felt Skye's hurt as well. "This isn't what I wanted. I just needed time, but now the truth is out, and I can't take it back. I love you. That doesn't change. I promise, Skye, I'll figure this out." I stepped forward, but my dragon pulsed inside me. I couldn't go any closer.

She just nodded but didn't meet my gaze.

I walked out and she slammed the door behind me. But unfortunately for my heart, my advanced hearing picked up the sounds of her dissolving into tears before I got into my car.

Damn it. I needed answers, and I needed them fast.

Chapter 21 - Skylar

Anthony disappeared—and I was *pissed*. I'd had a feeling he would pull some shit like this, especially after what had happened. I'd figured work would be awkward, but we were adults. We could've worked together without being bitter.

But Anthony had called the hospital CEO and put in for an emergency leave of absence, and nobody had batted a single damn eyelash about it.

And fuck all if I was going to go ask his parents where he'd gone. I considered asking Jace, but I couldn't bring myself to go anywhere near anyone in that cult.

Yeah, I said it.

I couldn't help but wonder if Sammy had anything to do with him leaving. I hadn't met the witch, but there had been a woman coming out of the administrative office at the hospital last week who definitely had a different energy around her. It was almost like I could sense people now. The announcement of Anthony taking his leave came shortly after I saw her there at the hospital. So, here we were, almost two weeks he'd been gone, and I'd settled my heart to believe it was eighteen years ago all over again. I tried to pretend I wasn't grieving. I knew he was probably off finding out what happened to those people in Washington, but he hadn't checked in, hadn't called or even texted. What was I supposed to think except that he'd gotten bad news and any day now I was going to have my memory wiped?

I didn't want to think that way. My mind just kept going to it, kept getting darker and darker. I left the hospital for lunch, as I had most days since Anthony had left. The last thing I needed right now was to run into Bret. That would've been the icing on the cake.

My new favorite place was this small café that I knew wouldn't be crowded during lunch. I'd be able to eat alone and in peace. I got my fancy sandwich and coffee and sat down in the corner, then pulled up a book on my phone. I hadn't been able to read any of those damn romance books, either. I was on a murder mystery. At least there were no fucking dragons in it.

Halfway through my sandwich, a woman flopped down across from me. Holy shit. It was the same woman who left the administrative office that day. And she still felt off somehow. I didn't have to guess. "Hello, Sammy."

She smiled. "Skye. You're as smart as you look."

"Are you here to wipe my memories?" I asked.

Sammy sat back in her chair. "I was ordered to."

My heart broke. Tears sprang to my eyes. I tried to keep them away but knowing that Anthony was going to make all the knowledge disappear, and all the feelings for each other, all the love I had in my heart for him, even though I was mad at him for disappearing again.

"Anthony didn't give the order," she said. "It came as a message from him."

I tried not to let the tears spill over. Blinking hard, I stared at the witch. "What do you mean?"

"I received the order second-hand. The clan isn't too keen on him disappearing with Jace."

I hadn't realized he'd taken Jace with him. Maybe he would be coming back eventually, then. I'd just assumed he'd gone alone.

And if he'd contacted me *at all,* I might've known differently.

"I'm feeling a little guilty," she said. "I gave them the nudge they needed."

"What are you talking about?" I asked.

"Anthony was looking for more couples like you, with no luck. Clans are very secretive and their witches are protective. If a secret as big as human pairings got out, it could send clans into a frenzy. Anthony seemed desperate, though. And he's my friend before he's my alpha, since I'm not a dragon. And so I used my power and resources and sent him to what I think, and hope, are the answers he seeks. Anthony's dad isn't happy with this news, but I was called by another member of the pack who claimed to be acting on Anthony's behalf. She wants your memories wiped before Anthony returns."

Why did this bitch hate me so much? "Tessa?" I asked.

Sammy cringed. "You've already had to deal with her?"

I nodded. "I don't know if it's jealousy or what."

"Fear," she said. "She's scared that human women will start taking all the dragons. If I have my way, she won't end up with anyone. She poisons anyone she comes near." She sighed. "She's also scared of change, but in that, she's not the only one."

"So, are you going to do as she's said? Are you obligated to?" I asked. I still had half my lunch in front of me, but my mouth was full of sawdust. No way I could've taken another bite.

Sammy shook her head. "Anthony is my alpha, and I don't see you as a threat. It's a part of my witchy gifts." She gave me a secret smile and stood. "I'm sure I'll be seeing more of you soon."

With that, she left the cafe.

Holy shit. My adrenaline crashed when Sammy was gone, and it was all I could do not to melt into a puddle there at the table. I gathered my trash and went back to work, ready to throw myself into my patients and to try not to think about fucking Tessa.

Hard as I tried, my emotions were mixed. I wasn't sure what to make of Sammy's visit. Should I wait for Anthony? Or was I wasting my time with all of this? Maybe it was time to cut my losses and move on. I just couldn't be sure.

As I walked into the hospital, I spotted Bret sitting on a bench looking like his entire world had just fallen apart. Damn it. Keep walking! But the soft part of my heart told me to check on him.

I stopped in the doorway and sucked in a deep breath. Damn it again. Turning, I walked to the bench beside the doors. "You okay?"

"Yeah," he said. His voice said otherwise, but who was I to argue with him?

"Okay." I turned to go back in.

"The baby isn't mine," Bret said in a voice damn near breaking down.

Oh, karma. What a slick bitch.

I tried *really hard* not to smile as I faced him. "What?" I managed to keep the grin off my face, but only just.

"Mary went into labor, and when the baby was born, it was quite obvious that he didn't belong to me."

I gave him a blank look. "Newborns can be quite deceiving. Their skin color can be skewed, and their little facial features distorted."

He snorted. "I asked and she confessed everything. She'd been seeing another man. She still has contact with him, and she's leaving me for him, since the baby is his."

I tried to pick my jaw up off the floor, but it didn't work. "Geez, Bret. That's pretty bad." About as bad as getting another woman pregnant a couple of months before our wedding, but I kept that part to myself. I tried to feel sorry for him, but the best I could muster was a pat on the shoulder. "You'll get over it, in time." I didn't make it a point to revel in the pain of others but damn if I wasn't lighting a candle when I got home.

He looked up at me with a broken gaze. "I'm so sorry," he whispered. "I shouldn't have taken you for granted. You were the best, brightest thing in my life and I ruined it. I should've waited for you to be ready to have a baby."

All the talk of babies made me pause. My cycle was pretty irregular, thanks to the PCOS, but I'd gotten good at timing them. If I stayed on a specific birth control, my periods were pretty regular. But if I went off that birth control, things went wonky, though I'd never gotten pregnant while off of it.

Now that I counted it up, I'd been due for a period over the past month. I stood in front of the hospital, in front of Bret, and tried to breathe. "I forgive you," I said absently. "All the best, gotta run."

Turning back toward the hospital, I didn't head for my floor. My patients would have to wait. I tucked myself into the bathroom and pulled my birth control out of my purse. Using my phone calendar, where I logged every time I started a new container of pills, I counted up how many should've been left.

Son of a bitch. I'd missed one. One pill too many.

With my stomach rolling, I exited the bathroom and went straight for the OB/GYN floor and grabbed the arm of a nurse I knew there, Charity. "Hey, can you squeeze me in for an appointment?" I asked.

She gave me a strange look. "Sure, what's wrong?"

I pulled her to the side. "I just need a pregnancy test."

"Well, shit, hang on. Those are a dime a dozen." She turned around and opened a drawer, then pulled out a white package. "Here, go do it now."

I snatched the package from her hand and ran for the bathroom. There was a little plastic cup by the sink. I grabbed one and followed all the instructions, dipping the little stick into my urine a few minutes later.

I set it on a napkin and read the instructions. Okay. Three lines was pregnant. Two was not. One was an error.

By the time I read that and looked back at the tiny stick... it had three lines.

Shit. Oh, shit. It had just been *one* pill!

How was this possible?

"Skye?" Charity called and tapped on the door. "You okay?"

I unlocked the door and peered out at her. "No, can you come in here?"

She bustled in, her hips filling up half the bathroom as I clutched her arm. She stared at the pregnancy test. "Yep," she said. "That's pregnant."

"How?" I asked weakly.

"Well, sugar, when a man loves a woman…"

"Stop it, Charity, you know I have PCOS."

She waved me off and patted my hand. "You know that not every case is the same."

That wasn't really what I'd meant, though she couldn't have known that. I was wondering how in the *hell* I was pregnant with a dragon's baby.

Charity went out to get a second test. I sat in a spare room and chugged a bottle of water. The thirty minutes that I played a game on my phone and waited until I thought I could pee again were the longest of my entire life. When I thought I could get enough urine out, I took it again and sure enough, three lines popped up within seconds. I didn't even need the full three minutes.

I cleaned up and washed my hands and shuffled out to the reception desk to make a real appointment. But shit, could I even use a regular doctor? Or was there some clan doctor I could go to?

The rest of my day passed in a fog. All my nurses asked what was wrong, but I kept blaming my behavior on not feeling well. Finally, it was time to go home where at least I could be alone and try to wrap my mind around the fact that I was pregnant…with a dragon baby.

When I parked, I didn't notice anyone on my porch. I was all the way on my front stoop before I saw Tessa sitting in the rocking chair beside my front door.

"What do you want?" I asked flatly.

She held up her hands. "I come in peace."

Yeah, right. My protective instincts ricocheted up to a hundred. This bitch was a danger and now I had more than myself to protect.

"You've got to come with me," she said. "Anthony's been hurt, and he needs your blood."

Fear pounded through me instantly. "What? How? Why didn't his parents come for me?"

She rolled her eyes. "Because they're going to him, idiot. God, you're stupid."

Well, that settled my suspicions a little. She wasn't trying to fool me by sweet-talking me. "My blood?" I asked.

"Mate blood has healing properties. If you're ever hurt, you need to get a transfusion of Anthony's blood and vice versa."

"Even though I'm human?" I asked.

Tessa stopped and looked confused. "Actually, I'm not sure. I assume so. We have to try, and we need to hurry."

"Fine," I said. "Where's your car?" I asked.

She rolled her eyes again. "I flew here, genius. We'll take your car. To Anthony's house."

I nodded and turned to go back to my car, but out of the blue, a cloud of dust surrounded my face. I turned back to Tessa in time to see her blowing the last of it off of her palm. "Sorry, not sorry," she said in a sing-song voice. "But I can't let you have him."

Damn it. "Baby," I managed to whisper before my body turned to jelly and the darkness overtook me.

Chapter 22 - Anthony

"Never thought I'd be so excited to see little Bluewater," Jace said as we entered the county.

I chuckled. "Me too. What a trip." We were almost home, and I was so excited to tell Skye what I'd found. It was all going to be okay.

After I'd gone to Sammy and pleaded my case to her, she'd relented. "I did some research, same as you did, same as your dad did, all those years ago when you found your mate," she'd said. "At the time, your father, the alpha, made me keep my research to myself. But he's not alpha anymore." She'd given us specific instructions on where to go and who to talk to and exactly what to tell them. It had taken some effort at the first location. They didn't want to give up their secrets, but once I explained the entire situation between Skye and me, they'd relaxed and given me the information I needed. They had a mated pair in their clan, a human woman, and a dragon man.

My energy buzzed higher the closer to home we came. I couldn't wait to see Skye. I was tempted to have Jace drop me off at Skye's place and he could drive my car home.

The woman in the first territory we'd visited, East Tennessee, she'd taken the bite and hadn't suffered any ill effects. She hadn't gone insane. She wasn't changed into a dragon, but they said she definitely had something more magical in her blood. Her health had been enhanced, and she'd actually been cured of the only medical condition she'd had: psoriasis. They thought that the magic of the bite worked like a cure.

I understood why they needed discretion, but it made me hopeful. Not enough to rush back home and risk it, though. We left Tennessee and went to the other three territories, taking turns driving to keep our time cut down. Still, it had been two weeks since we'd left Bluewater.

The other three territories gave me so much more information. They all had a human mate in their clan. All were safe. I'd never felt such relief in my entire life.

About ten minutes from town, my phone rang. I hit the button. "Hey, Sammy, what's up? We're almost back."

"Anthony, something's wrong."

My instincts went on high alert. Jace sat up and stared at the phone, even though Sammy's voice came out of the car speakers. "What is it?"

"Tessa came to me earlier today, telling me you'd instructed her to employ me to wipe Skylar's memories of the clan."

"I did no such thing. Tell me you didn't do it!" I gripped the steering wheel as my rage spiked and tried to drive sensibly.

"Of course not. But I wasn't sure where you were with the search, and I didn't want to bother you. I went and had lunch with Skye and decided she's not a threat to our clan. I let her know what Tessa tried to do and came home. Tessa called me to see how it had gone, and I told her the truth."

"I bet she didn't take it well," Jace said. I tried to laugh bitterly, but it came out as a growl. I was too angry and worried.

"Yeah, she kinda flipped. I've known her since she was a little girl and I've never seen her like that. She's always been catty and scheming, but this was off the deep end. She said she'd handle it herself. I rolled my eyes at first and started to let it go, but then I got worried. I called Skye's office, and she was still there working, so I waited. When I called them again and the office was closed, I tried her cell. I still had her number that you'd given me, so I tried to call, but it went straight to voicemail. I went to her house, and Anthony, there's something majorly wrong."

"What?" I yelled. "Spit it out!"

"I can't get in. I'm afraid to directly attack with magic because it might rebound on me. There's a sickly feeling in the air and a stench. I think Tessa's gotten her hands on an untied witch, one without a clan or coven. There aren't many witches that go without the protection and companionship of a witch family, but they are out there. Even rarer are witches willing to do this sort of magic without the sanction of a clan alpha or coven priestess."

"Get to the point, Sammy."

"The point is that I can't fight it with magic. You are going to have to come with muscle. There's a ward around the house! Get your ass here and fast because they're going to scramble this poor girl's brains."

I hit the gas and Jace grabbed the phone, switching it off of the car's system. "You focus on driving," he said.

We were close to town, but Skye lived several minutes past that. I drove like I'd never driven in my life. He spoke to Sammy in a low voice, ordering the clan warriors to report and meet us at Skye's.

We hadn't had any clan wars in hundreds of years, but as was tradition, we had a fighting force, prepared to assemble at a moment's notice.

I focused on weaving around slow cars and praying none of the police force was out. Jace hung up and made other phone calls, so he likely was warning our clan members that were officers. And sure enough, moments later, a police car pulled out in front of me as I rocketed down Main Street. I hated to take such a public route, but it was the fastest way to get to Skye. The car drove in front of me with the siren on and lights flashing, helping us clear the path to get to my mate.

"Tell him to turn off the siren. We want to approach as quietly as we can."

Jace pressed buttons on the phone again, and a few seconds later looked at me. "Got it. He knows." The sirens cut off far enough away that Tessa might think they went in another direction if she'd heard them from this far away.

I knew Tessa had a thing for me, but this was so far above and beyond anything I ever imagined she would do. I never thought she'd go to such lengths. She loved her clan. She had to know this meant major punishment. I wasn't even sure what I was going to do about this. It would depend on what Sammy could help me with.

As we got closer, the officer in front of us, I wasn't sure which one it was, turned off his lights. He pulled off on the road beside Skye's house but out of sight of her front windows. I went forward and parked behind her car in her driveway. I felt the magic before I stopped the car. Sammy was right. There was some sort of magical protection around the house. Jace made a gagging sound as we pulled up. "Oh, that's foul."

I threw it in park and launched myself out of the car, running hellbent for the front door. This felt like some dark, sick magic Tessa was about to use or was already using on my mate. The ward hit me like a freight train. I stopped short, nearly losing my breath as I hit it. Pushing forward, I strained against it. It fought me, but then the scent changed from foul, rotten eggs and sulfur to a bright spring day, like a field of flowers. I looked back to see Sammy standing in a defensive position, bent forward with her hands outstretched. Her icy blue eyes flashed as she groaned and fought against the magic. "Keep trying!" she yelled. "I'm just helping you get in!"

Cars began to pull up to the house, filling up the driveway and the road surrounding the area as dragons poured out of them. It wasn't just my warriors that had arrived.

My entire clan was here.

I turned, bolstered by Sammy's magic and the knowledge that I had the backing of what looked like all of my clan, and pushed forward.

This time, I was able to break through. The ward tried to steal my breath, but I pushed and pushed until I stumbled forward several steps, sucking in a deep breath of air.

As soon as the black spots faded, I ran to the door and slammed against it as I turned the handle. It opened easily.

As soon as I passed through, the stench of sulfur intensified about ten times. Tessa was in the corner of Skye's small living room and it looked like she was out cold.

A woman I didn't know stood in the middle of the room and Skye was laid out on the couch. The witch was totally focused on Skye, and the look in her eyes was pure greed. "I was going to just take her memories, take the money, and go. But then I smelled it on her." She breathed in deeper.

The witch stepped forward and blocked me from Skye as she bent over and put her hand on Skye's stomach.

The witch finally looked at me. "In all my years, I never knew a human could create life with a dragon. This is unprecedented."

My stomach dropped. Elation filled me, but it was chased away by terror. Skye was carrying my child, but the witch had her magic in Skye.

"I can only imagine the spells I could create with the mixed breed's blood."

I surged forward, ready to rip her head from her body, but she held up her hand.

"Don't move another muscle or you'll end up just like that little bitch over there. She tried to stop me when she found out about the spawn in this human's womb. I'm going to have this baby."

A glow surrounded Skye's stomach.

I wanted to shift, but the room was too small. I'd be likely to trample everyone.

There was only one thing a witch couldn't fight against: Dragonfire. But I wasn't that sort of dragon. I channeled water, not fire. But it had been known to happen.

My dragon couldn't speak to me. It wasn't that sort of relationship. He wasn't a sentient being. He was a part of me. But thoughts of trust washed over me, and I let my dragon take the lead.

He was raging inside me, anyway. I wasn't sure how much longer I could've held him off.

I didn't want to hurt Skye, but I had to get the witch away from her. My throat shifted, and something inside me did as well.

This time, it was painful. Partial shifts weren't really supposed to happen. Part of my inside turned, and fire rose up my throat. It burned as it went, but I let my dragon do what he needed to do, and he fired a shot of pure dragonfire at the witch. I didn't really want to hit the witch, but for it to be enough to get her to back away from Skye.

It worked. She turned toward me and jumped back, luckily closer to the front door. I shot fire again, catching the curtains alight right over Skye. But I could get her out, first I had to get this witch out of the house.

The witch was pissed. She screamed and sent spells at me, but I kept shooting fire at her until she backed out of the house. Then I crowded her.

"Sammy!" I yelled. "Get Skye out and make sure nobody can see us!"

"*Kill her!*" she screamed, telling me we were covered. I watched as Jace and my dad fought against the ward. They'd get Skye and my baby out.

The witch sent another spell my way, which I ducked. It hit the house, catching another spot on fire.

Enough. I shifted fully into a dragon, filling up the front yard and breathing more fire toward the witch but away from my family as they tried to get in the house. I had an idea and lifted my head, directing a pure, white-hot stream of flames at the ward.

It had the intended effect. Jace and Dad let out grunts as the ward disappeared and they fell through.

Good. Now I could give the witch my full focus.

If a dragon could grin, I would've. She shot spell after spell at me, but my hide protected me. She tried focusing on my face, the most vulnerable part of me, but the fire kept melting the spells before they struck.

The downside was that producing the fire depleted my energy at an alarming rate. I didn't want to take a life. As a doctor, I'd spent all of my adult life fighting to save all the lives I could. But I couldn't see any other way around it.

I focused on the witch and opened my mouth again. With a mighty roar, I blasted her with the hottest, thickest dragonfire I could muster. It encompassed her, lighting her on fire immediately.

Her scream, the horrific sound of her dying, would be a sound that would stay with me until the day I died.

The witch's magic burst from her and hovered in the air, wild and unstable. Sammy rushed forward. "Go," she yelled. "See to Skye!"

She turned and did something, waving her arms around, but I didn't have time to see what it was. I turned to find Jace carrying Skye out of the burning house and my dad carrying Tessa. We rushed out into the yard, well away from the fire.

The rest of my clan shifted. Sammy did something and started yelling. "Shift! Use your waterpowers!"

In minutes, the dragons had shifted, and water flowed from my clan onto my mate's house. I didn't care about that right now. If she were well, I'd build Skye a million houses. I only worried about what was happening inside her. I collapsed in the side yard beside her, where Jace carefully set her down. "Skye," I whispered.

Sammy rushed over and dropped down between Tessa and Skye. She put one hand on each of them and closed her eyes. Shuddering, she moaned and stiffened, but then seconds later, both Skye's and Tessa's eyes opened.

Sammy leaned forward and retched into the grass as both Skye and Tessa gasped and sat up.

I gathered Skye into my arms and began to sob. "I'm so sorry," I said into her shoulder. "I should've been here for you."

She patted me on the shoulder. "What in the hell happened?"

I didn't have words to explain it. I felt silly, the big bad alpha sobbing into his mate's hair, but I couldn't help it.

I was that relieved.

Chapter 23 - Skylar

My house reeked of smoke. I sat at my kitchen table with a cup of tea that someone had put in front of me. I couldn't remember coming home. The last thing I could bring to mind was being at the hospital, shocked at the news I'd gotten at lunch. I realized my hand was on my stomach and jerked it away before the rest of the people sitting around the table noticed.

Tessa sat across from me, looking like guilt personified. My house was totally wrecked. In my daze, I couldn't muster much grief for it, but I knew myself, later on, I'd be upset about some of the things that had burned. Books on my bookshelf beside the front window. My curtains that had been Dad's. And I loved that sofa, just a pile of ash now.

Members of Anthony's clan moved furniture out as we sat, and I tried to wrap my mind around everything. Anthony's mom sat beside me with one hand on my back. "Darling, are you sure nothing hurts?" she asked.

"Yes, but I need to go get something checked out," I whispered. I wanted an ultrasound. I needed to make sure the baby was still there and there was a heartbeat.

Sammy tapped the handle of the teacup. "Drink that. It'll bolster you up, and the babies, too."

I stared at her in shock, my gaze darting from her to Anthony, and then his parents. "The what?"

Anthony mimicked me. "The what?"

Sammy's eyes widened. "I thought you knew," she whispered and covered her mouth. "You didn't know you're pregnant?"

"You did?" I asked. "And you said babies, plural."

She nodded. "Yes, I sense two distinct souls in there."

My jaw dropped. "No, no way. I only found out today. I haven't even had time to tell Anthony or my dad!"

"Well, they're healthy and strong." She reached over and patted my shoulder. "And the tea will help, so drink up."

I pulled the cup to my lips with shaking hands and drank. It was tasty, at least.

"Are you okay?" Anthony asked. "Really?"

Sammy smiled. "Well, I gotta run. You two don't need me anymore."

"Are you sure?" I whispered.

She just winked and looked at her bare wrist, as if she were checking her watch. "Gotta go!"

"I'm fine," I said, answering Anthony's question. "I just want to know what the hell happened."

He nodded. "Right, well, let's get sorted. Mom, Dad, can you see to locking Tessa up until we know what to do with her?"

Tessa moaned. "I'm so sorry," she whimpered. "I thought I was helping you."

Anthony glared at her. "You were trying to help yourself. Get out of my sight."

His dad squeezed his shoulder and they left, marching Tessa between them.

"Couldn't she just run away?" I asked.

"I don't think she will," he said. "Come on. Let my clan work on your house. We'll have it back as good as new in no time. In the meantime, will you stay at my place?"

I looked at my destroyed living room. Part of the wall had burned totally through. It was going to need so much work. "Yeah, I'll stay with you."

My only other choice was staying with Dad, and I could always do that if Anthony pissed me off or didn't have a really damn good explanation.

I downed the rest of the tea now that it had cooled and felt a little stronger almost as soon as I finished it. I made a note to remember to thank Sammy later on.

After some finagling of cars, since most of Anthony's clan was still at my house, he extracted my car and drove us straight to his place. As soon as the door shut, I started grilling him.

"What happened?"

He grimaced. "Today or over the last two weeks?"

I had a good idea of what had gone down today. "Start at the beginning."

"We've been on the road nonstop. I've been texting you every night, but you never replied. I just knew you were so mad at me that you'd never speak to me again when you never replied."

I held up one hand. "Hold on. What do you mean every night? I haven't gotten a single text from you!"

He leaned over and dug his phone out of his pocket with his eyes on the dark road. I wasn't sure when the sun had set, but it was pitch black on the quiet beach road now. "Look for yourself."

Hey, he suggested it, so I went for it. I scrolled through his messages, glancing only briefly at the ones that didn't apply to me. Under my name, there were dozens of messages.

We're halfway to Tennessee. Stopping for the night. I miss you.

Got some encouraging news in TN! More when I'm surer. Miss you.

Please just text me and let me know you're okay.

Miss you.

Love you.

We'll figure this out, Skylar, please believe that.

They went on like that. Short, but so sweet. "Anthony, I didn't get any of these," I exclaimed. "I wouldn't have felt so abandoned the last two weeks! After the first couple of nights, I cooled off and really worried about where you were. I only sent you one text, out of stubbornness, I guess, but never got a reply."

I held up my phone when he stopped at a stoplight. All I'd sent to him was, **I miss you.**

"Check the phone numbers," he said as he waited for a car to pass in front of us at the four-way stop and then he went.

I clicked his name on my message to see the phone number. "207-555-6238."

"My number ends in 6239. Now check your number in my phone."

I looked, and sure enough. "Mine is off by one digit, too." I changed it and then fixed his number in my phone. "I'm assuming Tessa did that," I said, my voice nearly matching the severity of Anthony's when he did his angry growling thing.

"I'll find out," he replied.

I sighed and leaned against the seat. "So, you got good news?"

"Yes, I visited four clans that all had a human living amongst them, who had taken the bite. They had zero complications. When I told them about the woman in Washington, they were shocked. The only conclusion any of us could come up with was perhaps they weren't really fated, and the dragon was mistaken about the direction of his affections. I don't see how that could happen, it seems unlikely he'd be confused about who his tattoo burned for. But two of the clans I visited knew of other instances of the mating that were not their secrets to tell. They told me they were not in America, so I know they weren't the same clans I went to see. Those clans also had success. So, if the Washington clan's experience was a true one, and it is possible, we have a one in seven chance of you not responding well to the bite."

"Still," I whispered. "That's pretty scary." I watched the darkness glide by while Anthony drove us closer to his house. "What happened at my house? I don't remember going home or anything."

"We know you finished your day at work. Sammy kept calling and figured out when you went home, but she got here after you did, and by then they already had you inside and Sammy couldn't break through. I'm not sure another dragon could have if it weren't for my dragon being so desperate to get to you and Sammy helping me fight the magic. I got in and ended up breathing fire to defeat the witch, which is what destroyed your house." He glanced at me, but I couldn't see his face well in the dark. The instrument panel on my car didn't provide enough light. "I'm sorry about that. I'll make sure they fix it up good as new."

"It's okay," I whispered. "They're only things." But it was starting to set in that my home was half-destroyed. "Wait, did you say you breathed fire?"

"Yes, there are documented instances when non-fire dragons can produce dragonfire. And I was one of them. I'll have to tell the other alphas at our annual meeting," he mused.

I laughed. "You have a meeting?"

He looked at me quizzically. "Of course. How else do we keep up with news of our cousins and stuff? We usually rent a large swath of cabins out in nature somewhere, or one clan will host all of the other clans. It's chaotic and loud and messy and our favorite time of the year."

"You'll have to do that then," I said, picturing what it would be like to have all the other dragon clans descend on us here in sleepy Bluewater.

He pulled in front of his house, then ran around to open my door. Thanks to the tea, I felt pretty normal, so I laughed at his efforts. "I'm barely pregnant, Anthony."

"Well, get used to this. I'm going to make sure you don't have to lift one unnecessary finger during this pregnancy."

"Twins," I whispered. "I can't believe it." And I probably wouldn't until I saw it on an ultrasound screen. "Oh, that's another question. Can I have regular doctor appointments? Can I do ultrasounds and bloodwork and all of that?"

"No to the bloodwork," he said. "We have some basic lab equipment that belongs to the clan that we can use to check most things, but the advanced testing that a lot of women have done is out of the question for dragons. But you can go to most appointments, have ultrasounds done, and all of that. But if you want, I could be your doctor. I'm more than willing to buy the clan an ultrasound machine, anyway. The women have been begging for one."

I grinned. "I do know how to use one."

How cool would it be to be able to see my baby anytime?

"Tell me about the witch," I said as Anthony made me settle on the couch and put my feet up. He covered me in a blanket and grabbed all the pillows in the house, it felt like, to get me up and comfy. "I'm fine."

"She was just going to wipe your memory and move on, which would've been violating enough and cause enough for me to banish Tessa forever, but once she discovered your pregnancy, the witch decided she wanted the baby. I don't know if she was going to try to kidnap you until you were full-term or somehow speed up the pregnancy and make you deliver now? I have no idea. I killed her before she had the chance." He paused and closed his eyes. "That was not something I ever expected to do, but I did what I had to do to keep my family safe."

I smiled and rubbed my stomach, pushing aside the trauma that was going to come from Anthony having killed someone. "I don't suppose you have a clan psychiatrist?" I asked. "You may need to talk to someone."

"No, but I can find one in another clan and do a virtual visit." He shrugged. "Not a bad idea, really."

"This is why secrets are important. I can't allow anyone in the clan who could hurt us, which now includes you and our baby. Babies." He wrinkled his brow and laughed. "Babies."

I shook my head at him. "I don't trust Tessa. I'm not sure what to do with her." I didn't have the first clue how to handle this. It wasn't like we could go to the police and demand she be arrested for trying to perform a spell on me. They'd lock us up in the loony bin.

"Mom and Dad will keep her under lock and key. We'll worry about it another day. For now, I want to focus on you."

We spent the rest of the day discussing the future. All the what-ifs. And by the end of the day, we knew that me taking the bite right now wasn't a possibility.

"I think my dragon will stop riding me so hard to bite you. It's like that part of me realizes how dangerous it could potentially be for the babies. I don't feel a strong urge like I did before. I can't say for sure what I'll feel when we have sex again, but I don't think I'll be pressed so hard to bite you."

I beamed at him. "I want to take your bite," I said. "I want to be your mate. But you're right. Not until after." It might've been impulsive and a little too soon, but I knew it was right. Nothing about it felt bad or wrong. My very soul wanted to be Anthony's mate.

We discussed everything from where we wanted to live, to baby names, to how involved our parents would be. And oh, shit, I still had to tell my dad.

I stayed with Anthony all week. Then he convinced me to call out of work because like someone had flipped a switch, exhaustion set in. We both knew from our OB/GYN rotations during residency that one of the most potent first trimester hormones could cause extreme exhaustion. After what I went through with the witch, we both felt better safe than sorry. He went back to work and covered all my shifts while I stayed home.

I was never alone, though. His mother came, as did Sammy. I got to know both of them so much better and found myself more and more excited about the coming babies. Karah, in particular, was ecstatic. "You have to understand how much I'm going to spoil those children," she said.

We made plans, then changed them, then thought up some new ideas. We decided to move into my place, then back to Anthony's, then to build an entirely new place. Then back to Anthony's, then mine. It was so much fun, as the possibilities were truly endless.

Saturday, my girls showed up out of the blue. "I've got a meeting," he said with a wink. "And all of my family will be there, so I called in reinforcements." He grinned and left as Bri and Kaylee walked in and ran over to hug me. Then Bri's daughter slipped out from behind her and grinned at me. As Bri settled her at the coffee table with a coloring book and a fresh pack of crayons, I thought about what it was going to be like to be a mother, finally, and started bawling.

Of course, they wanted a lot of answers. They wanted to know if we were back together first, and what about it made me cry?

"I'm pregnant," I exclaimed.

Kaylee burst into tears and hugged me. "I know how much you've wanted this," she whispered. "I'm so happy for you."

Bri smiled at us. I looked at her over Kaylee's shoulder. "You're going to be a great mom," Bri said.

"How does Anthony feel?" Kaylee asked.

I chortled through my tears. I didn't know how to answer honestly without telling too much. "He's feeling very overprotective."

They knew he'd taken off again. I didn't really have an explanation for them, so said the first thing that came to mind. "He had a friend in trouble. It's not my story to tell, but he explained it all to me and I've forgiven him. We also discovered that Tessa bitch had altered our phone numbers. She admitted to sneaking around and doing it the night we were all at Jace's bar. I don't know how she managed it, but it kept us from communicating, which made both of us think the other was angry. Apparently, she had some major boner for Anthony. He's told her off now, so hopefully, she won't be a problem in the future." What an understatement.

When Anthony came back and they left, he told me where he'd been. "I wanted to surprise you with your friends," he explained. "Or I would've told you about the meeting. I just spent the entire day talking to my clan about you and our babes. I expressed in no uncertain terms what would happen if anyone spoke on you and our babies. I love you, Skye, and I love those babies inside of you. I'll do whatever it takes to keep you all safe."

"What about Tessa?" I asked.

"She's got a lot of guilt," he said. "She's going to go spend some time with the Tennessee clan, and hopefully come back with a better mindset. For the time being, Sammy was able to perform a spell that prevents her from shifting. We hope that will be punishment enough, but we'll see how she acts when she returns. I didn't want to deprive her of being around her family forever, so this was the best solution I could come up with. It's not like I can remove her ability to shift completely."

I nodded. "I think that's fair. You said that once she found out I was pregnant, she tried to stop it. She was willing to mess with my memories, which to me is inconceivable, but among your kind, it's just something that is done. I don't know how I feel about that in general, but I can't hold her to a stricter standard than the rest of you."

"Maybe it's time to reflect on our stance on that as well," he said. "That is certainly something we can address in the future." He leaned forward and pressed a kiss to my forehead. "Things are due for a bit of a shakeup anyway."

"For my part, I decided before that you're my person," I said. "You always will be."

He pulled me into his arms and hugged me close. "And you're mine," he whispered. "Always."

Chapter 24 - Anthony

My new home wasn't big enough for Christmas dinner with the whole clan. But my parents had built their house with the knowledge that they'd be hosting dozens of people at once, so their entire downstairs was an open floor plan. Therefore, Skye and I were hosting Christmas for the clan at my parents' house, and it was going great. Everyone was having a great time, except for poor Skye. She'd crossed over into the *extremely* pregnant range. And even though we'd forced her into my mom's favorite comfy recliner as soon as she'd arrived, and the women of the clan had taken over babying her and making sure she had anything she could desire, she was so huge and miserable. I wished, not for the first time, that we were like seahorses. Seahorse males carried their young. I would've taken the pain and discomfort off of my mate in a heartbeat.

Sammy was floating around somewhere, mingling with the clan, and my mom was in the kitchen, constantly cooking something. We'd done potluck and buffet style, and everyone ate all night rather than trying to have tables to seat everyone at once.

Out of the blue, Skye went from laughing at something Jace said to gasping, and Sammy appeared out of the blue. "It's time," she said excitedly.

The atmosphere in the house turned electric, and everyone turned to look. We all felt it.

"Okay." I held my hands up. "We're ready. Let's get her to our place and get this show on the road."

Sammy squinted at Skye. "Nope," she said. "No time. These babies are coming now."

"Do we have time to go upstairs?" I asked as Skye cried out.

"Holy shit," she yelled. "This hurts!" She took in a few breaths. "Someone call my dad!"

"Quickly," Sammy said.

"I'll call him," Dad said as I lifted Skye into my arms and hurried up the stairs to my old bedroom.

Mom followed and squawked. "Hold on!" She scurried to a hall closet and pulled out a shower curtain in the package. "We'll put this under her."

I chuckled and held Skye in my arms as she whimpered and mom spread out first the curtain and then ran from the room and came back with a bunch of towels and handed me my travel medical bag, which I hadn't gone anywhere without since Skye had entered her third trimester.

About five minutes after Skye let out her first gasp, we had her on the bed in her sports bra and nothing else. I settled beside her and used my medical training to check how dilated Skye was. "Shit," I whispered. "You're at ten."

Her eyes widened. "How?"

"I might've helped," Sammy said. "Sped things along so you don't have a long, drawn-out labor. Now, let me in there and I can help with the pain, too."

She settled beside Skye on the bed and put her hand on her belly, and Skye's face went from twisted in pain to relaxed. "I still feel pain but it's more annoying than overwhelming." She breathed several times. "Thank you."

Sammy beamed at me. "You ain't seen nothing yet. Dr. Daddy, do your thing, then I'll help again."

"You know the drill," I told Skye. "Push when you feel the need." I stayed between her legs and when she had a contraction, Sammy and my mom helped her lean forward. In minutes, the first baby was out.

"Holy shit," I breathed. We had opted not to find out the sex. My mom left Sammy to help Skye and rushed around to wrap baby number one in one of her big, fluffy towels. I cut the umbilical cord and almost immediately, Skye began to push again. This was unlike any birth I'd ever been at. I glanced at Sammy, who had a triumphant look on her face.

"Is this you?" I asked.

She nodded. "I'm handy at birth."

"That's why all the clan moms have you come," Mom said as she looked at the first baby in wonder. "It's a girl." She sucked in a shaky breath as tears coursed down her cheeks.

I touched my face to find tears there as well. My daughter sucked in a deep breath and began to cry with me as I guided the second baby out. We'd finally have a female alpha.

Skye was a trooper, and a few minutes later, Mom gasped. "It's a boy." She sobbed and laid her head on Skye's shoulder. "Great job, Mama."

A little boy. Tears rolled down my cheeks in earnest now. "Are you sure you know what you're doing?" I asked Sammy.

She scoffed as I handed Skye our little boy, wrapped in a towel. I focused on the babies, checking them over, and making sure they were safe and sound. Both were as healthy as I'd seen any newborns, and like all dragon babies, came out human.

My tears fell when they each opened their eyes, and they were gold.

"They're dragons," my mother whispered. She was looking at our little girl over Skye's shoulder as Sammy worked between Skye's legs.

Mom ran from the room to tell the clan, and Skye gasped. "What did you do?" she asked.

"Sped things up," Sammy said. She wiped her hands on a towel and started cleaning up the dirty towels that had accumulated during the very quick delivery. "Her healing is more like a week out. The uterus is mostly shrunk back down, and she didn't rip or tear, thanks to me, but she should continue to heal with only mild discomfort." She put her hand over each of the twins, proclaimed them healthy, and left, leaving us all in a state of shock and wonder. It was done. We had our twins, one of each, and the future of the clan alpha lineage was secured.

Less than an hour after it all started, we were in the spare bedroom in my parents' home with our babies in our arms.

"Wow," I whispered. "Did that really just happen?"

Skye burst out laughing and tears coursed down her cheeks. We stared at our children in adoration for several minutes until Mom popped back in.

"What are their names?" she asked. "And can the grandfathers come in? Your father just got here, along with your girlfriends. I sent most of the clan to finish the party at your beach house," she said. "Sammy's heading there now to provide a bit of cover."

I grinned. They'd finished Skye's beach house the month before and we'd decided to keep it as a sort of second home. She'd generously offered it up to the clan as well. If we had anyone visit or if any members of the clan needed a temporary home, they were welcome to it.

It had endeared her to them even further. I couldn't have loved her more already.

We argued for several minutes over names as our visitors filed in and out. "How about strong names like Artemis and Athena?" I suggested, deadly serious.

Skye burst out laughing, as did my mother. "No," Skye said. "Absolutely not. How about Sean Mitchell, after our dads?"

Her father was in the corner of the room, holding our little girl, and looked up in awe. My father stood uncomfortably, being out of his element in a birthing room around babies.

I gazed lovingly at my son. "Are you Sean Mitchell?" I asked him. He nuzzled me. "I think he likes it."

"I know I do," Sean said. Smiling, I looked at Skye's father. We'd had a moment the first time I saw him after moving back to town. He was a man of few words, and had basically told me as long as I treated Skye right, we had no problem.

I stood and put my son in my father's arms. "What do you think, Gramps?"

He beamed, and something in his face changed. I knew he'd never be the same.

"Okay, you can name our daughter then," Skye said. "But please, for the love of all that's holy, no Greek goddesses."

Sean stood and handed me my daughter. "Let me hold my namesake," he said proudly. He and my father squished together so they could each gaze upon the little boy named for both of them.

I stared down at the wrinkled beauty in my arms. "How about we keep the same initials. Star, since you're my Skye, my princess can be my star. And Mia after my mom's middle name." I would've liked to have named her after Skye's mom as well, but she'd taken off on Skye when she was a little girl. She didn't even remember her.

Skylar burst into tears. I couldn't help laughing at her raging hormones, even as I slipped onto the bed and pulled her into my arms. She took Star and cried into her blanket, which my mother had produced from nowhere.

I wondered how many other baby items she had tucked away. We'd planned on waiting and buying the bulk of it after we knew the sexes. I imagined there wasn't much we'd need to shop for, knowing my mother.

***

I didn't know how life could've gotten any sweeter, but two months later, it did. I came home from work to an empty house. "Hello?" I called as quietly as I could.

The babies were usually up around the time I came home and Skye either would have her hands full or one of the grandparents would be here helping out. Once my father had gotten a load of his grandkids, it had been difficult to keep him away. But no one was there.

I bounded up the stairs. Maybe everyone was asleep.

But no. Skye was waiting for me in our bedroom. "Hello there," I said. It was hard not to realize the reason the house was empty but for me and Skye. Candles lined every surface, and the bed was covered in rose petals. "Hey," I said. "No more babies. Not anytime soon."

Skye gave me a knowing smile. "I'm tired of waiting, Anthony." We hadn't had any time alone since the babies were born. She'd had more than enough time to heal up.

She stepped closer, pressing her hands to my chest. Her vibrant green eyes peered up at me through her long lashes. "I want you."

A hungry growl ripped through my chest as I pressed her flush against me, claiming her soft, pliant lips. I'd done the responsible thing by not pressuring her for sex while she healed, but I'd be lying if I said I hadn't been impatiently waiting for that day. She wrapped her arms around my neck, and I scooped her legs up around me.

"Are you sure you're ready?" I asked. "I don't want to—"

"Yes, Anthony. I'm more than ready." Her reply was a breathy whisper. "Make love to me."

I wasn't about to argue that. However, I knew I'd need to be gentle. She was the mother of my children, the love of my life, and even if she was fully healed, I wanted to be careful. I set her down lightly on the rose petals she'd scattered across the bedspread. Between that and the candlelight, she looked almost ethereal.

The silk robe slipped from her shoulders, exposing her bare form. Her breasts were fuller, her stomach still receding from the ordeal of having carried not one, but two babies, but she was still the most beautiful woman I'd ever laid eyes on. I clenched my jaw down on the urge to mar the perfect flesh of her shoulder and neck.

Instead, I took a fistful of silky brown hair and gently tilted her head back. The skin of her throat tasted of my citrus body wash and, combined with the vanilla of her shampoo, made for an alluring blend. I ran my hands across her heavy breasts, kneading them lightly. They would likely be sore for a while yet, but I wouldn't dare complain about our limitations.

Trailing my fingertips lightly across her skin and down her belly, I was met with wetness. She was more than ready for me. She gasped as I brushed over the sensitive nub, back arching toward me instinctively. Her legs spread wider, giving me easier access, and I took it.

My fingers slid along her slick folds and she leaned back on her hands. I followed, lavishing the column of her throat with my attention. Her hips moved in time with my fingers and her breaths became rapid and uneven. I nipped lightly at the delicate flesh where her throat met her shoulder, even that little bit proving to be almost too much for me to hold back. She whimpered, pulling me closer.

"Do it, please."

Pulling back, I studied her face for a moment. I wanted to, more than anything. The need to bite and claim her was overwhelming. But there were risks.

"Sammy came to me earlier," she confessed. She ran her thumb across my cheek with the hand that wasn't holding her up. "She said she *saw* it, and it's time. Everything is going to be okay."

If there was anyone I would trust with Skye's life, it was Sammy. The two of them had grown really close. If Sammy saw our mating and knew everything would turn out fine, then I would trust that.

"Okay," I whispered.

She tugged my shirt off and tossed it over her shoulder. I pressed her back onto the petal-covered bed, then slid off the edge to the floor. Knowing that I was going to do it settled the intense need I had to get it over with. First, I'd need to bring her close. Not that I hadn't dreamed of tasting her womanhood again for weeks already.

Skye's hips jerked at first contact. I applied pressure to her clit, then slid my tongue back to her opening. She groaned and gasped, muscles tightening. Her fingers found my hair and I skimmed mine along her slickness before easing them inside her.

Her back arched up off the bed and she clenched tight around my fingers. I needed to make sure she was prepared to take me again, so I kept pumping them in and out leisurely while my mouth worked the rest of her. Watching her writhe under my loving attention had me loosening my pants and pulling them down as far as I could from my position on my knees.

"Please, Anthony." She tugged on my hair impatiently. "I need you in me."

Ignoring her pleading, I sucked her clit into my mouth. She cried out, hips bucking against me. Damn, I'd missed that. When her tugging became painful, I relented and backed off with one last stroke. I stood and kicked my pants away, crawling up beside her on the bed, leaving a trail of kisses all the way up, especially on the fading stretch marks.

"Okay, love," I said. "Just tell me if it hurts too much."

She nodded, running her fingernails through my hair. That feeling sent a chill down my spine every time, it felt so nice, and my cock twitched in response. I pressed my forehead to hers as I rubbed it against her, coating it in her fluids. The friction was torturous but so good. Finally, I positioned myself at her entrance and eased inside her.

I watched her expression carefully for any signs of pain but found only love and lust in her eyes. Slowly at first, I started moving, her hips trying to keep time with mine. The feel of her around me brought back the temptation to sink my teeth into her. Her breathy moans urged me on, and I picked up the pace just a bit.

"Faster, please."

Who was I to deny this woman anything? She knew her body, knew what it could handle. I could give her what she wanted, at least.

My speed increased again, and I kept a tight lid on the part that enjoyed the brutal, unyielding pace she'd so enjoyed in the beginning. It wasn't the time for that. Her core muscles tightened, her breath coming in pants, and I knew she was close. Judging by the heat building low in my stomach, I was nearly there as well.

Instinct took over then. My nose grazed over the tender spot around her collarbone. Fangs extending, I bit into her flesh. Magic exploded over us, through us, exponentially increasing our pleasure long enough to crash through orgasm together before it all finally settled. I could feel the moment our bond snapped in place between us.

I drew back, pleased to see how little blood there was. Licking over the wound, I watched as it healed before my eyes. As soon as the last mark sealed, my clan tattoo materialized across her shoulder as my tattoo burned again for the first time since we'd decided to be mates. It flared for a second, then faded away.

Skye gazed up at me adoringly, and I leaned down to kiss her.

My mate.

Chapter 25 - Jace

"Have a good night!" I called to my last customer, a regular. He stumbled out the door. I knew he lived in the small apartment complex down the road and that he'd drive home. I'd also been careful to serve him no more than he could handle. I didn't want to deal with a passed-out dude on the sidewalk. The cops would bring that shit back to me, for sure.

I grabbed up a full bag of trash and walked it out the back door, slinging it over the top of the dumpster. As I was about to shut the back door, I heard a muffled cry. It was definitely female and in distress.

I stopped and listened, tuning in to my preternatural hearing. The sound came from way back in the alley, nearly behind the building. I crept forward and after a few more seconds, heard more.

The stench of fear hit me hard, though. "Leave me the fuck alone." The voice was feminine, small, and absolutely terrified. Even if I couldn't smell it, I heard it loud and clear.

"Did you think you could run away from me forever? I will *always* find you, bitch. Who do you think you are, taking my daughter away from me? Did you think I'd just let that go?"

"No, but you can't do this. I have a restraining order against you." She cried out, and that was all I could take.

I rushed down the alley. I couldn't stand by and let this guy hurt this poor woman. I burst out and found them around the back of the building, just outside the rear entrance for the small nightclub next door. They must've exited from there.

I shoved the guy away and turned to the woman, and as soon as I touched her, a searing pain shot across my arm.

"Shit," I whispered. It was unlike anything I'd ever felt before. The pain was both intense and manageable. I looked down at my arm to see faint lines of a tattoo begin to appear. Son of a bitch.

"Get your hands off of her!" the guy yelled. He was clearly drunk and belligerent. As he came at me again, swinging at me wildly, I easily ducked him.

Shit. I hated dealing with cops, but if anybody needed to be arrested, it was this douchebag. I shoved him hard, so he went down on his butt. "Stay there, asshole!"

I kept my phone in my back pocket and pulled it out to call the police. I kept my arm around the shaking woman and finally got a good look at her. She looked familiar. "Here," I said. "I called the Bluewater PD. Tell them what's going on."

She nodded and took the phone I'd held out to her. "Thank you."

The drunk tried to get up again, but I snarled at him. He stayed on the ground.

The good news was that she didn't try to protect her apparent abuser. She told the cops everything. "My ex-boyfriend found me. I've been hiding from him. I've got a restraining order against him, and he just tried to hurt me."

She rattled off where we were and handed me back my phone.

"Thank you," she whispered.

I nodded absently, looking at her, then my arm.

The cops got there quickly, one of them being my buddy, Ian, who was another dragon in our clan. I gave my statement, as did the woman, who I learned was Briana Wallace, age thirty, one daughter, a local teacher. She didn't know how the asshole found her and was terrified that he'd find her daughter, who was safe at the house of her friend, Skylar.

That explained why she looked so familiar. She always came in with Skye and their tattooed friend. Her other friend, the one with all the piercings, she was more my speed. This woman, Briana, would've been the last person I expected to be *my* fated mate. And a human, too…Come on.

I was raised by a single mother. Dragons didn't often have broken families, but they did exist, and I came from one. I knew too easily what this woman was feeling. It was one of the reasons I'd chosen not to take on a mate. I didn't want to end up being like my asshole father. But it didn't stop me from wrapping an arm around the shaking woman as she cried and gave her statement. Ian asked her what she was doing out so late. "I had a girls' night out with my friend Kaylee."

Kaylee, that was the name of the other friend.

"I was headed to my car after getting some coffee from the diner. I hadn't drunk anything, but I was really tired, so I wanted a little caffeine for the drive home. Kaylee went home with her current boyfriend and I found my ex waiting at my car. I ran from him, which was stupid because he cornered me back here."

Ian closed his notebook. "Okay, you don't have any visible injuries, but you can file a private suit against him for breaking the restraining order. We'll take him in for a drunk and disorderly for tonight. You can pick up your report tomorrow."

He gave me a sympathetic look and glanced at my arm. When he saw the tattoo there, his eyes widened, and he turned to Bri again. "Do you have someone you can stay with?"

She nodded. "My best friend has two houses. She'll let me stay at her spare."

She meant Skye and Anthony's beach house; I was sure. She stepped away as Ian left and sucked in a deep breath.

"Thank you so much for stepping in and helping me," she said. "I don't know what he would've done." She picked up her purse from the ground. "I've gotta go get my daughter and leave. I guess we can't stay in one place for too long."

My arm burned hotter. Son of a bitch! Skye and Anthony opened the damn floodgates with dragon and human mating in our clan and now I couldn't stand the thought of this woman leaving alone. But she was a human. How was this possible? I mean, I knew it was possible, but the likelihood of it happening to two of us in one clan was unheard of.

"Are you leaving?" I asked. "Like, leaving town?"

She gave me big eyes that made me want to rip the drunk's head from his shoulders. "I don't see what choice I have."

Motherfucker. I tried so hard to mind my own damn business, but this time I couldn't. This slip of a woman, this *teacher* was my fated mate. And I couldn't let her leave Bluewater.

What in the fuck was I going to do now?

Printed in Great Britain
by Amazon

16978858R00241